RAKING HELL

A body is wrapped in a bloodstained horse-blanket. A farmer admits to the gruesome crime, but with good reason. So will the sheriff arrest or protect the guilty man when eight men come looking to settle the score? After all, the sheriff has taken an oath to protect the town . . . This story of judgement, consequence and the promise of retribution, tells of one man — Sheriff Will Price — who is prepared to go raking hell to fulfil his pledge . . .

LEE CLINTON

RAKING HELL

Complete and Unabridged

LINFORD
Leicester

First published in Great Britain in 2011 by
Robert Hale Limited
London

First Linford Edition
published 2012
by arrangement with
Robert Hale Limited
London

The moral right of the author has been asserted

British Library CIP Data

Clinton, Lee.
  Raking hell. - -
  (Linford western library)
  1. Sheriffs- -Fiction. 2. Western stories.
  3. Large type books.
  I. Title II. Series
  823.9'2–dc23

  ISBN 978–1–4448–1057–8

Published by
F. A. Thorpe (Publishing)
Anstey, Leicestershire

Set by Words & Graphics Ltd.
Anstey, Leicestershire
Printed and bound in Great Britain by
T. J. International Ltd., Padstow, Cornwall

This book is printed on acid-free paper

For the two JHs —
one got me writing,
the other got me published.

For more information about
the author of *Making Hell*,
please visit www.leeclinton.com

1

With Forethought and Malice

Monday 3 June 1878 — Just Before Noon

The body was wrapped in a horse blanket stained dark with blood and tied tight by rope around the feet, waist, and neck. The binding with its neat knots drew the heavy brown fabric into the shape of a big solid man and, as the corpse was pulled from the horse, the weight came upon the three deputy sheriffs by surprise. One stumbled backwards and fell unceremoniously upon his backside in the dirt. He got up quickly, dusted himself down, then looked around with embarrassment but no one was paying him any attention. All their eyes were on the large body that now lay upon the ground, a

1

macabre sight, still bent in the middle from where it had hung across the horse for its journey to Eureka Falls. It now seemed to be half sitting in the road outside the sheriff's office, legs outstretched, head and shoulders leaning back as if ready to lie down and sleep.

The crowd continued to stare upon this peculiar sight as a young boy asked his mother for an explanation but received none. He asked again, curious and enquiring, what was it they were looking at?

'Quiet, child,' came the stern reply.

The admonished youngster pressed his face against the folds of his mother's dress and bit at his thumb as the sheriff stepped from his office to gaze down upon the bound figure.

'Jeezus,' he said under his breath. 'Lonny, get the undertaker.'

The deputy's eyes glanced up in acknowledgement before he turned and started to walk up the street.

'Quick, Lonny.'

The deputy slowly quickened his pace into a lazy run towards John W. Wilks & Son, Funeral Directors of Eureka Falls.

'Nothing to see here folks,' said the sheriff. 'You should all go about your business and let me and the deputies deal with this.' He looked down at the young boy, then to the mother. 'And this is no exhibition for youngsters.'

The mother turned, her hand behind the head of the child, guiding him away as the onlookers slowly dispersed. But they did so while glancing back and bumping into each other.

'Who is he?' asked Sheriff Will Price of the two remaining deputies while his eyes remained fixed on the corpse.

'Victor Kerry,' came the reply, but not from either of the deputies.

The sheriff had to step off the veranda to see that the voice had come from behind the three tethered horses. 'And you?'

'Joseph Bunny.'

'You care to explain, Mr Bunny?'

'Not a lot to explain,' said the lean man with the knotted veins in his sinewy arms. 'This is the body of Victor Kerry. I killed him yesterday, before noon, then wrapped him up in one of his blankets and bought him into Eureka Falls on his horse to turn him over to the law. He is now your property.'

'Why Eureka Falls?'

'It was where Kerry was heading so I completed the journey for him.'

The sheriff looked around at the loitering crowd, their faces showing keen interest in the conversation they were straining to hear. 'I think you better come into the office, Mr Bunny, and tell me exactly what happened. I take it, it was self-defence?'

Joseph Bunny continued to ease the harness on one of the horses, pulling down on the belly-strap as the leather made a stretching sound before the brass buckle clinked and released. He patted his hand against the tan rump of the horse then rubbed it gently in a circle.

'Nope. Not self-defence. I killed Victor Kerry with forethought and malice.'

2

A Diamond Ink Mark

Monday 3 June 1878 — Noon

'Where are you from, Mr Bunny?'

'Can I sit?'

'Yes, you can sit.'

Joseph Bunny wiped his hand across the seat. 'Dust,' he said as he sat, his hands showing grazed knuckles and dried blood.

'Where are you from?' repeated the sheriff.

'Over near Lake, back in the valley, east near the plains towards Cheyenne Wells a little. Near — '

Sheriff Will Price interrupted. 'I know the country, so what are you doing down here on this side of the mountains?'

Bunny leant back in the chair,

shifting his weight as he settled and relaxed. 'I'm only in your neck of the woods because that's where Victor Kerry was heading. Had he gone west to Crowley, then I'd be speaking to the sheriff there.'

'Your occupation?'

'Farmer. Just a small property but enough for one man. Cattle, sheep' — Joseph Bunny gave a faint grin — 'and pigs.'

'You find this amusing?'

'Nope, not particularly.' Bunny stretched out a leg and placed a hand on his knee and began to rub in small circles. 'You know who I am; you know where I am from; you now know what I do for a living, but it seems like a lot of beating around the bush. So, let me answer the questions you seem reluctant to ask.' He bent then straightened his leg as the knee cracked. 'That doesn't sound good does it? Sometimes I swear it squeaks when I walk, specially on early mornings when the air is cold.'

Sheriff Price said nothing as he leant back against the edge of his desk but the tight grip of his knuckles showed his annoyance with the man before him, and Joseph Bunny noticed.

'I tracked Kerry south down the Big Sandy Creek,' said Bunny his voice calm and even. 'Thought he was heading for Lamar at first. He didn't know I was on his trail and was riding slow and leaving clear tracks. I caught up with him the night before last and got him by complete surprise. He'd been drinking a little, corn liquor from a jug, and that made it easier I guess but I still had to take him on, head to head.' Bunny stretched out the other leg. 'This knee is fine; it's just the right one that gives me trouble. Lucky I guess that it's not the other way round or I'd never get on or off my horse.'

The sheriff's knuckles strained white. Bunny grinned just a little.

'I killed Victor Kerry because he killed my brother's wife, Heather Bunny, week ago Tuesday. She has the farm next to mine and when I got back from fixing a fence up the valley I went over to see her. Found her in the back room just before she died.' Bunny spoke slowly and the grin was gone from his face. 'She had been forced upon and was bleeding real bad. Kerry had tried to strangle her after the act as well as hitting her on the side of the head with an oil lamp. I thought at first she was going to survive, but then she just seemed to give up after telling me what happened.' Bunny shook his head. 'Maybe it was the shame of it all. It left her with no dignity and our Heather was a lady with pride.' Joseph Bunny looked up at Sheriff Will Price, his eyes cold and grim. 'She was also a good farmer. A better one than my brother.'

'How did you know it was Kerry who did it?'

'Ain't too many men that look like Kerry; besides, Heather saw the ink mark on the back of his right hand, a diamond and the word, Moose. I believe that's what he is called by his associates and I guess it's because he's as big as a moose.' The slight grin returned. 'There's a scarcity of men who look like Victor Kerry with a diamond on the back of the hand and the word Moose. It was him all right, of that there is no doubt.'

The sheriff nodded as he moved his weight and crossed his legs, his grip on the desk relaxing a little. 'So, how — '

Bunny noticed the sheriff's stance before he replied. 'How did I know where he was going, so I could follow?'

The sheriff nodded again.

'I went to the sheriff of Lake City and told him what our Heather had told me. He knew of Kerry and had seen him that day getting drunk, so he and his deputies checked out the saloons but they couldn't find him. The next morning he was seen at the back of Stanley's Livery Stables, still drunk and trying to saddle his horse to leave. I felt relieved that they had got him and was ready to head home, but the sheriff said I should stay, to give evidence.'

'So what happened?'

Bunny leant forward. 'Some people got cold feet. Victor Kerry has powerful friends and the good leaders at Lake felt the chill, especially the mayor who told the sheriff to let Kerry go. He said Lake didn't need or want any trouble.'

Will frowned in disbelief. 'And?'

Bunny slumped back into the chair in silence.

Sheriff Will Price asked again. 'And then what happened?'

'Kerry rode out of town a free man and justice rode out with him, while I went back to my property. But I didn't stay. I took my good horse and one of Heather's, packed enough supplies for ten days and set out after him on my own.' Joseph Bunny shrugged his shoulders. 'And I caught up with him and killed him. That's it.'

The sheriff spread his fingers on the edge of the desk and looked around the office not wanting to make eye contact. His feet scraped against the floor as he drew himself upright to stand. 'Is that it?'

'Yep.'

Sheriff Will Price shook his head, his eyes still avoiding him.

Bunny stood, slowly flexing his right leg three times before he put his weight on his foot. 'Sheriff, you look a little confused. Why don't you telegraph the sheriff at Lake and tell him I arrived on your doorstep with the body of Victor Kerry and that you want to verify my story of the rape and murder of my sister-in-law. That will give me a chance to water the horses, wash up and rest my knees.' He leant down and rubbed his right knee. 'That's unless you want to lock me up straight away but I'm not planning on going anywhere, so you've got plenty of time.'

The sheriff looked uneasy but nodded. 'I'll do that, Mr Bunny, that's exactly what I'll do. I'll also have you hand over all weapons, and your horses are to be impounded in our stables. One of my deputies will show you where. You are not to leave town and you are to be available at any time I need to speak to you.'

'So you're not going to lock me up?' Bunny looked down the narrow passage towards the back of the office where a small single iron cage was located. It was full of furniture along with a mop, bucket and broom. 'I'll clean it out for you, if you want?'

'That won't be necessary, for the time being.'

★ ★ ★

Why Sheriff Will Price never arrested and locked up Joseph Bunny for the murder of Victor Kerry has never been fully explained. After all, Bunny had confessed to what he had done, but Will Price always did things his way and was never one to explain why, even to the mayor. Maybe it was the circumstance — a simple farmer avenging the brutal murder of a close relative. Or maybe it was just the size of Victor Kerry against that of Joseph Bunny. Kerry was a bear of man, while Joseph Bunny was lean and of medium build. To take on Kerry would have required a high degree of courage no matter what the reason.

Then there are those few men who knew Sheriff Will Price well and may have offered another reason. The sheriff of Eureka Falls had a good nose for judging men and a keen sense of justice, and maybe he thought justice had been delivered and that it didn't need a court of law to tell him that. But for whatever reason, the sheriff let Joseph Bunny, who had admitted to the murder of Victor Kerry, go and water his horses.

3

Who was Victor Kerry?

Monday 3 June 1878 — Early Afternoon

The sheriff dipped the nib of the pen into the ink well and began writing on the yellow telegraph pad.

To the Sheriff of Lake City
From the Sheriff of Eureka Falls
This day Mr Joseph Bunny a citizen of near Lake City arrived at Eureka Falls with the body of Victor Kerry. In investigating the circumstances surrounding Kerry's death I request any information that may have a bearing on the situation. Your earliest response would be appreciated.
Will Price

The telegraph clerk read over the page, counting each word with the point of his pencil that left small dots on the form, before he scribbled the number of words in the box at the bottom of the page, along with the date. 'I guess you want this sent as a priority?'

'I do, thank you, Aubin.'

'I can mark it urgent.'

'I don't know if it's . . . ' The sheriff paused, silent in thought for a moment as he placed the pen back in its holder. 'That would be fine, Aubin. Urgent.'

'Means they not only get it quicker but that they also answer quicker,' said the telegraph clerk as he pencilled the word URGENT in bold letters at the top of the form.

The sheriff nodded in agreement and when he returned to his office he took Deputy Logan Pitkin to one side away from the other two young deputies. 'Lon, does the name Victor Kerry mean anything to you?'

'No. Should it?'

'It was the body that was bought in by Mr Bunny. He says Victor Kerry murdered his brother's wife last week. Seems he tracked him down then killed him.'

The deputy let out a 'phew' sound in amazement. 'On his own?'

'Seems so,' said the sheriff, keeping his voice low.

'How?' asked the deputy.

'Didn't say but I expect he shot him.'

'Expect so,' repeated Deputy Pitkin. 'Need a buffalo gun though. That was a big man wrapped in that horse blanket. It put Doogan on his rump when we were getting him down.' The deputy smiled.

'Lon, I want you to sit down and go through the *Law and Order Gazettes* and see if you can find the name Victor Kerry, or the nickname Moose, Moose Kerry.'

The deputy turned to leave, eager to start.

'Just wait, Lonny.'

Pitkin turned back to face the sheriff with a look of having been chastized.

'I don't want rush, I want accuracy.'

The deputy went to speak but the sheriff kept talking. 'Also I want you to search out if there is any mention in the gazettes about any group or gang that uses a diamond as their motif.'

'Motif?' The deputy seemed confused.

'Decoration. Seems Victor Kerry has a diamond-shaped ink mark on the back of his right hand.'

The deputy was nodding his head vigorously.

The sheriff caught his deputy's eye. 'Accuracy, Lon, remember accuracy. Now, you can use my desk, it has more space to spread out the gazettes.'

The deputy showed his delight at getting to sit at the sheriff's desk then wrinkled his brow. 'Where are you going to sit?'

'I'm going up to see Cyril Wilks. I want to find out the cause of death of Victor Kerry and get his height and weight. I also want to see this diamond mark.'

'When is he going to be buried?' asked the deputy.

'Don't know yet, I'll talk to Cyril. Seems he was killed yesterday, just before noon, so no hurry. Don't know if someone will want to collect the body.'

'You think someone might come for the body?'

Will Price rubbed two fingers across the groove in his chin. 'Maybe, maybe not, but before we either release or bury Victor Kerry I want to know who are his powerful friends.'

'Powerful friends?' repeated Deputy Sheriff Lonny Pitkin.

But the sheriff didn't answer as he grabbed his hat and opened the door to leave. He was a man with urgency in his pace.

4

A Gruesome Death

Monday 3 June 1878 — Mid Afternoon

The sheriff's mind was preoccupied with thoughts of Joseph Bunny and Victor Kerry and didn't hear Cyril Wilks, the Eureka Fall's undertaker, calling. 'Sheriff, Sheriff.'

Sheriff Will Price kept walking, head down, shoulders hunched forward, his pace quick.

'Sheriff,' called Wilks again from the far side of the street, as he broke into a run of short quick steps.

The sheriff looked up just as Wilks's hat fell from his head. The short round man stopped, put his hand on his bald head then looked around for his hat, now directly behind him and lying on the ground.

'Cyril, I'm on my way to see you.'

'And me to see you, Will.' The undertaker was flustered and now out of breath.

The sheriff picked up Wilks's hat. 'Is it important?'

'It is.' Cyril was panting in small sharp breaths.

Will Price waited for Wilks to elaborate but there was just silence. 'You going to tell me why, Cyril?'

Wilks looked around at two women with their small children, who were standing on the boardwalk in front of the haberdashery store and watching. 'Best done back at my office,' he said, keeping his voice low.

'Is it to do with the body?' The sheriff now looked towards the women and also lowered his voice. 'The body that arrived in the horse blanket?'

'Yes it is.'

The sheriff handed the undertaker his hat. 'Your office then, Cyril.'

'Mervan is there too.'

'Merv Larson?'

21

'Yes, he sent me to get you,' said Cyril. 'I called him in to inspect the body and determine the cause of death. As soon as he saw, he said I should get you immediately.' Wilks put his hat on his head, his face still flushed. 'Grisly business. Never seen anything like it in my life.'

Merv Larson was the town physician — an elderly man who had seen death in all its forms over his long years in practice. When younger he had worked on ships that sailed from the length of the east coast and beyond, into English and French ports delivering cargo — mostly cotton and later treacle from way down south.

'Huge vats of the stuff,' he had told Will. 'Weighed a ton and could kill a man if they came free in a heavy sea.'

And Merv had amputated appendages when at sea — fingers, hands, feet, arms and legs from cargo mishaps. Sometimes doing his grisly business in the hole of a heaving ship under the light of a swinging lamp, to free a sailor who had become pinned between the cargo and the bulkhead. It was this knowledge that had made him invaluable as a battlefield surgeon when in 1862 General 'Old Brains' Halleck recruited him and put him to work.

During the Vicksburg Campaign he had spent six weeks amputating limbs where lead shot had smashed and splintered bones, to leave arms and legs twisted and hanging limp and lifeless. Then, after that, when Confederate General John Pemberton surrendered, to heap 30,000 prisoners of war upon the thin means of the small band of physicians. By war's end he had seen every possible wound and every echelon of suffering, so he headed west in search of the quiet life and stumbled upon Eureka Falls.

'Doc,' said Will, as he pushed the brim of his hat up an inch in the dim light of the undertaker's office.

'Sheriff,' responded Mervan who was seated at Cyril's desk, filling out a form.

'Be with you in a minute, just need to finish this.'

When Mervan placed down the pen and stood, Will could see that he had an apron on, the top half had been untied from around the neck to now hang from the waist. 'Cyril says you wanted to see me. Immediately.'

'Yes, you better come and have a look at this, Will.'

The large room at the back of the office was cold and dark except for the yellow glow of the oil lamp that hung above a table. Silhouetted on the flat bench was the figure of a large man on his back with his feet hanging well over the end, making the table look short and small. The body was naked but covered from the waist down by a cloth, the face showing a full beard.

'Big man,' said the sheriff.

'Yep, six foot seven and half inches and weighing over three hundred pounds.'

Will tilted his hat back again so that

he could see a little better. 'I believe he's got a mark on the back of his hand. An ink mark.'

'That's right. Here,' said the physician, as he pointed to the right hand, 'a diamond, along with the word Moose.'

Will leant in close to take a look, then slowly stepped back to view the huge body. 'Not someone you would want to pick a fight with, eh?'

'No,' agreed Mervan. 'He's a goliath.'

'So how did he die? I take it he was shot but I can't see any marks or any blood?'

'Well, he has been cleaned up. There was plenty of blood, but no marks on the upper body where you'd expect a man of this size to be shot. And I would have thought more than one shot would have been required, even with these modern cartridges. I'd say two or three at least but there was none.'

'So how did he die?'

'Well, he bled to death.'

'From what wound?'

The undertaker stood silent and

motionless next to Mervan, his face grim.

'Down low; I'll show you.' Mervan pulled the cloth from the body and handed to Cyril who took it and began to fold it neatly.

The sheriff leaned in close to inspect the lower part of the body as Mervan pulled the overhead lamp to the side to cast a better light.'

'Jeez,' said the sheriff. 'Jeezus, he's been castrated.'

'No, it's more than that. He's had everything removed, all of the genitalia, and do you know why I know he's had everything removed?'

Will nodded his head. 'I can see. There's nothing there.'

'Yep, that too, but Cyril found it all in the pocket of his jacket, wrapped real neat, in grease paper.'

'Jeezus,' repeated the sheriff.

'You want to see?' asked Cyril, the folded cloth now hanging across his arm.

'Hell, no. I'll take your word for it.'

'It must have been a gruesome death,' said the physician. 'Question is, who would be so brave or foolish to try to do such a thing to a man of this size? And I have to tell you; the cut is as neat as you would like to see. This has been done by a skilful man, someone who butchers their own livestock, I'd say.'

The sheriff stepped back and nodded. 'Cattle, sheep — ' He paused and then said, 'Pigs.'

Mervan nodded in agreement. 'You know him?'

'Yeah, met him this morning — a farmer from over near Lake City by the name of Joseph Bunny.'

5

Squealed Like a Pig

Monday 3 June 1878 — Late Afternoon

The sheriff found Joseph Bunny at the Apple Blossom Boarding-house, sitting on the edge of the steel bed with his boots off.

'Good boots,' he said. 'Even better off than on.' He grinned as he looked up.

Sheriff Will Price did not. 'I've just come from the undertaker's where I inspected the body of Victor Kerry with the town physician. He has listed the cause of death as bleeding.'

Bunny rubbed his right knee and flexed his toes in a sock that had been neatly repaired at the heel with blue darn. 'Yep, I can vouch for that.'

'You want to tell me why?'

'Thought I had. He raped and murdered our Heather.'

'Why didn't you just shoot him? Would have been easier.'

'Yep, easier, but that would have been too humane.'

'You think he deserved to die like that?'

'Wouldn't have done it if I didn't.'

The sheriff seemed lost for words and the awkwardness of his silence filled the small room.

Bunny shifted his weight on the edge of the bed and the wire springs creaked as he kept rubbing his knee.

'Sheriff, if you want to know all the details I can tell you, but I don't know what good that will do.'

'How did you get — ' Will searched for the words. 'Take advantage of such a big man?'

'I caught him by surprise and as I told you he'd been drinking.'

'I've dealt with big drunks and they can still cause a lot of trouble, even for two or three men, especially if cornered.'

'Bulls are big and I handle them fine.'

'He wasn't a bull, he was a man.'

'He wasn't as smart as a bull and I'm good with a rope, so I roped him.'

'And after you did it? That putting his . . . '

Bunny bent his leg back and scowled as the knee clicked. 'In his pocket?'

The sheriff nodded.

'I like to keep things neat and I wanted to show it to him. I wanted him to see what I had done, so I gave it back to him and put it in the pocket of his jacket.'

'For God's sake, he was a man not an animal.'

Bunny stood up and his chest expanded as he drew in a deep breath, his eyes locked on to Will's. 'He was an animal and I did to him what I do to animals. You should be thanking me. Victor Kerry was heading for your town.'

The sheriff could see the steel in

Bunny's eyes and slowly shook his head as he turned to go.

'Sheriff, he had his opportunity to take me down,' called Bunny. 'I tracked him and he took no evasive action, but I still had to use my wits to get in close. Before I could rope him I had to grab him and when I went for him I was stripped down, with no gun. He had his, a .45 Schofield, better than my old Remington, so I had one chance, just one chance, and I took it.'

The sheriff stopped to listen but didn't turn his head.

'If he'd had his wits about him,' added Bunny, 'he could have taken me easily with that Schofield. It looks brand-new, and a fine handgun, but he wasn't smart. He was just a violent man who could frighten those who couldn't, or wouldn't, defend themselves.'

The sheriff stepped off again without saying a word.

'And I've got to tell you, Sheriff, for a big bull of man, when I cut him, he squealed just like a pig.'

Sheriff Will Price stopped and turned. 'How long did it take? You said you killed him yesterday before noon, but you also said you caught up with him the night before last.'

Bunny looked defiant. 'That's how long it took and, if you ask me, it was still too quick.'

6

Be Cautious

Tuesday 4 June 1878 — Mid Morning

Aubin Mead walked from the telegraph office down the boardwalk to see the sheriff. In his hand was a buff envelope.

'I brought down a telegraph form too. If you want to reply, I can wait.'

'Thank you, Aubin.' Will waved a hand towards the long bench seat on the other side of the small counter.

'No, I'll stand, thanks, Sheriff. Spend too much time sitting as it is.'

'You and me both.' Will slid his thumb under the envelope flap and pulled it free. Aubin turned away and looked over to where Deputy Lonny Pitkin sat at the sheriff's desk with a pile of gazettes.

Will opened the single sheet of paper and began to read.

To the Sheriff of Eureka Falls
From the Sheriff of Lake City
Joseph Bunny known to me personally as an honest but sometimes abrupt man who has suffered a recent family loss, including the death of his sister-in-law, Heather Bunny on Tuesday May 28. Victor Kerry, also called Moose Kerry, believed responsible. Kerry, a known associate of Black Jack Carlson, was considered dangerous. I was obliged to advise Carlson of the death of Victor Kerry as he was departing this morning to return to Cheyenne Wells. I believe that he and his associates are now heading your way. His intentions are unknown but I urge you to be cautious.
Wes Nettleton

Will folded the telegraph and placed it back in the envelope.

'Reply, Sheriff?' asked the telegraph clerk.

'No, not at the moment, Aubin.'

'I'll go then.'

Sheriff Will Price was deep in thought as he rubbed two fingers across the cleft in his chin.

'I said, I'll go then.'

The words seemed to wake the sheriff. 'Right. Thanks, Aubin, thank you for walking this down to me, I'm much obliged.'

Before Aubin Mead reached the door he heard Will Price call to Deputy Pitkin.

'Lonny, tell me what you have found in those gazettes on Victor Kerry, and I want you to search for what we have on Jack Carlson. Black Jack Carlson.'

The sheriff slowly reopened the envelope and withdrew the telegraph as if for the first time. He then laid it on the counter and where it buckled at the fold, he smoothed it flat with the palm of his hand and read it again. When he finished, he read it for a third time and finally again for a fourth before he looked up to see Deputy Logan Pitkin standing beside him with an armful of gazettes. Strips of paper protruded from the pages with hand-written notes that showed he'd been busy with his research.

'Sheriff, I'll start with what I've found so far.' Lonny dumped the pile of gazettes on to the counter. '*Law and Order Gazette Volume 32, MDCC . . . .*' Lonnie was reading out the roman numerals for the year of the gazette.

Will lifted a hand to stop him. 'Lonny, just give me the gist of what you have found with dates and places I can understand. Then you can point me to where I need to read.'

'Right. Right, Sheriff, but I don't have much for you to look at. I've searched hard but I have found little.'

'That's fine, Lonny, but it doesn't mean you have to string out what you've got. Just give it to me straight.'

'OK, but I only have one reference.' The deputy then added, 'So far.' He let out a small cough to signal he was ready to present his report. '1871, Colorado State Penitentiary, 11314

Kerry, Victor J. Incarcerated for cattle stealing. Given six years but released after serving five years and one month.'

'That's it?'

Lonny looked a little hurt as he nodded a yes.

'OK. That's good, Lonny.'

Lonny's hurt look turned into a smile.

'So he has a record,' continued Sheriff Will Price. 'And we now know that he was in the State Penitentiary from '71 to '76 and it looks like he had been out of trouble for the last two years, maybe, until he killed Heather Bunny last week. And we now know he is deceased because we have his body here in Eureka Falls.' Lonny shifted his weight from one foot to the other, nodding his head wisely as Will made his deductions. But Will wasn't paying attention to Lonny. He might have been talking out loud but he was talking to himself. 'And we now know that he is associated with someone called Black Jack Carlson who is heading our way

37

with a number of others. To do what? Collect the body of Victor Kerry? Or . . . ' Will touched his chin. 'Or . . . '

Lonny looked confused. 'Sheriff?'

Will didn't hear. 'Or are they coming after the man who killed Victor Kerry. Mister Joseph Bunny.'

'Sheriff?' repeated Lonny.

The sheriff was looking around the counter now littered with gazettes. 'Where's that telegraph form that Aubin bought with him?'

Lonny looked down. 'There, Sheriff, near the envelope.'

Will took up a pencil and began to write.

To the Sheriff of Lake City
From the Sheriff of Eureka Falls
Please advise as to Black Jack Carlson and any associates who may be travelling to Eureka Falls and of their time of arrival.
Will Price

'Lonny, get this up to Aubin to send

off as urgent, then I want you to continue searching the gazettes for any word on Jack Carlson. Try State Penitentiary records for 1871 to 1876 first.'

Before Lonny could respond, Will had grabbed his hat and was heading for the door.

'Where are you going, Sheriff? Sheriff?'

Will was at the door as he called back over his shoulder, 'To speak to Joseph Bunny.'

7

No Pity Tuesday

4 June 1878 — Noon

Sheriff Will Price found Joseph Bunny over at the livery stables brushing down one of his horses. Will stood some distance back at first, watching the lean man skilfully work the brush in long strokes down the front leg, grooming with care. When he approached the stall he did so quietly, still observing as the brush made a swooshing sound against the shiny tan coat.

Joseph Bunny spoke without turning his head. 'This one loves the brush,' he said, as he bent low to continue the long strokes.

Will was of a mind to avoid small talk but a voice inside told him to slow down, to change his approach. Why? He couldn't say but maybe it was some of his grandfather's advice from long ago, who told a young Will Price that, 'When a man speaks he is telling you something — even when he just seems to be passing the time of day. So remember to listen.' Or it could have been the gentle actions of a man caring for his horse, a man who had violently killed an opponent almost twice his size and weight just days before, and then admitted it to the law with honesty. So, Will drew in a long slow breath and decided to chat to Joseph Bunny.

'Don't they all? I know all our horses like the brush.'

Bunny smiled but it was unseen by Will. 'Yep, I guess they do at that. Bit like people. People like to be stroked from time to time. I don't mind doing it to animals but not to humans.' Bunny stopped and straightened up, turning to Will. 'But you didn't come to chit chat with me about grooming, did you, Sheriff?'

'No I didn't, Mr Bunny. I came to ask you about other things.'

Bunny turned back to his horse and continued to brush. 'And what would that be in particular?'

'Jack Carlson.'

Bunny kept brushing.

'You know of him?' continued the sheriff.

'Oh yes, I know of Black Jack Carlson.'

Will clenched a fist in annoyance at Bunny's preoccupation with the grooming of his horse; he wanted him to stop, to turn and face him so they could have a proper conversation. But his grandfather's voice from long ago whispered in his ear. 'Let him tell it his way and in his own time.'

Will flexed his fingers. 'I'd be obliged if you would tell me what you know, Mr Bunny.'

'My name's Joseph,' said Bunny. 'Not Joe mind you, my mother was particular about that. I wanted to be Joe when I was a young boy, until I was eleven, then when she died I only wanted to be called Joseph.'

At least he's talking, thought Will. 'Joseph,' he said and stopped to listen.

The silence hung in the air except for the swoosh of the brush against the horse. Bunny leant in close, his cheek touching the coat. 'Jack Carlson calls himself a businessman and runs a syndicate out of Cheyenne Wells but he also has considerable interests in Lake City. Cattle mostly but it's big business and he has his finger in a lot of pies, including a large property called the Blue Diamond.' The brush strokes were now a little quicker. 'Then he started lending money to local businesses, just small amounts to start. He helped Seb Hoffman expand his hardware store with a new storehouse at the rear. Then Glen Riley got to put in a new oven at his bakery, and even Des Emmet took out a loan to buy some stock, from Carlson, of course. That's when it started to get in my way.' The brush strokes now came fast. 'That's when

Linton, my young brother, did the same and borrowed money without saying a thing to anyone. Heather came and saw me when she found out. She was concerned and didn't like the idea of going into debt and nor do I. I don't like owing any man and certainly not the likes of Black Jack Carlson, but it was too late; Linton had signed the papers and joined half the folk of Lake who now owed money to Carlson.' The brush strokes were vigorous. 'Best part of a year went by. Then Black Jack decided to foreclose on the contracts everyone had signed. They all held a clause that allowed for him to be repaid within thirty days on demand, or he could take what was his due as a percentage of their businesses. Some of the smart ones sold what they could real quick, paid up and got out of the contract, but that was less than a handful. Vernon Fraser at the First National did what he could to help by refinancing some, why I don't know because he had warned most of them that borrowing from Carlson came with a risk. For most, like Linton and Heather, they had nowhere to go. They were caught.' Bunny stopped brushing. 'Half their farm now belonged to Carlson and immediately he started charging rent.' Will saw Bunny's hand stop and grip the brush tight. 'What they had to pay each month in rent no longer made their farm workable.' The brush moved again slowly. 'Victor Kerry told Heather that he had been sent to collect that month's rent for Carlson, but it was the first time she had seen him. Carlson sometimes collected but mostly it was an older man who rode around with large saddle-bags full of the monthly rent takings. But Kerry turned up last week and pressed himself on our Heather.'

'Where was your brother, Linton, your sister-in-law's husband?'

Bunny's body seemed to shake slightly. 'Young Linton hanged himself in the barn last Christmas Eve.'

'I'm sorry,' said Will.

Bunny turned. 'I'm not.' His words were soft but bitter. 'He got Heather into this mess then left her to fend for herself. You may feel sorry for him but me, I don't, I ran out of pity long, long ago.'

Will rubbed a finger across his chin. 'I telegraphed the sheriff at Lake City and he vouched for you as an honest man and I believe that to be so. But I now believe that you are in danger as Jack Carlson and his associates have been told of the death of Victor Kerry and are heading to Eureka Falls.'

The sheriff expected Joseph Bunny to stop, turn and face him on receiving the news he had just been given, but he continued to brush his horse and smiled. A smile unseen by Sheriff Will Price.

8

A Conflict of Interest

Tuesday 4 June 1878 — Afternoon

Will Price was on edge when he arrived back in his office. When he spoke to Deputy Logan Pitkin he was abrupt, then silently cursed himself for the indiscretion. 'Give the gazettes to me,' he had said, 'and I'll find out if there is any citation on Black Jack Carlson.'

He found it in twenty minutes, in an 1873 list of internees at the Colorado State Penitentiary: 11973 Carlson, Jack W. on a charge of fraud and embezzlement. He had been given two years and six months but was released after serving two years and two months. 'In 1875,' he read out loud to himself.

In his mind, Will ran back over the facts and tried to make sense of it all.

The revelations by Joseph Bunny and the endorsement of honesty from Sheriff Nettleton at Lake City, all had the ring of truth but the situation regarding the business dealing of Jack Carlson was new to him. He'd had no idea that such a scheme of money lending existed and especially at Lake City that was only a two-day ride away, nor had he read of any such matters in the *Law and Order Gazettes*.

When Will paid a visit to Wilfred Hislop at the Eureka Falls Branch of the First National Bank, the story that Joseph Bunny had told was now repeated by the bank manager in alarming detail.

'Very sorry state of affairs,' said Wilfred, 'and not good for Lake at all. Many of those debts were big, long-term affairs and while they would have eventually been paid off, Carlson foreclosed. Trying to then refinance the loans was always going to be difficult.'

'I've never read about any of this in the gazettes,' said Will.

'Why should you? Carlson hasn't broken any laws, all the loan contracts were above board and legal. It was just that those who signed them didn't read the fine print. When he evoked the clause to foreclose on the loans, all those who had borrowed money from him had signed the contract agreeing to a thirty-day provision to pay up on demand. It really upset a lot of people when he lay claim against their assets but there was nothing they could do.'

'So how many got stung?'

'Near on half the town I guess, from what I've heard.'

'So, does that mean that Carlson owns half of Lake?'

'In a fashion, but it could be worse than that.'

'Worse? How worse?' asked Will.

'In the banking business, when you lend money, it's not just how much you lend but who you lend to.'

'And?' The confusion on the sheriff's face showed and the bank manager saw it.

'I'll explain, but I tell you this in strict confidence and because you are our sheriff.' Will nodded his acceptance that what he was about to be told would be held in good faith. 'I've been told that the mayor and most of the town council are in debt to Jack Carlson but that he didn't foreclose on them.'

Will was stunned. 'The mayor and most of the councillors owe Black Jack Carlson?'

'Yes; it's not a good situation for the town of Lake, is it? The civic leaders owing a man like Black Jack Carlson.'

'But how can they still hold positions of office? Isn't there a conflict of interest?' asked Will.

The bank manager put his thumbs into the pockets of his waistcoat. 'Well, yes, technically but it's never been put to the test and until it is, then they could argue that they have never given him favour.'

'Until now,' said the sheriff.

The bank manager's face showed

concern. ''Til now, you say?'

'Let me now tell you something in confidence. One of Carlson's associates was involved in a heinous crime over near Lake last week, death of a woman who was in debt to Carlson. She was able to describe her assailant before she died and Sheriff Wes Nettleton was able to apprehend him. But ... ' Will paused and rubbed his chin. 'But it seems that the mayor told the sheriff to let him go, which he did. That man then started heading for Eureka Falls.'

'You think we should be concerned?'

'From what I'm starting to learn, very concerned.'

'So when will this man arrive?'

'He's here, arrived yesterday in a horse blanket with the man who killed him, the brother-in-law of the mur- dered woman.'

'Oh,' is all that Bank Manager Wilfred Hislop got from his lips.

'But that's only half of it. Black Jack Carlson and his associates are now on their way to Eureka Falls to, I guess, collect the body and find out who killed him.'

'Oh, shit,' said the grey-haired bank manager.

Will looked at Wilfred in surprise. In the twelve years he'd known him, not once had he heard a word of profanity pass his lips.

9

Arrest and Protection

Tuesday 4 June 1878 — Late After-noon

Aubin Mead walked the telegraph down to the sheriff just before five o'clock. Will was in the office on his own when he was handed the buff-coloured envelope, but this time the telegraph clerk didn't offer to stay and wait for a response; instead, he hurried to attend to other business and seemed a little agitated.

Will propped the envelope up against the inkstand and attended to the loose papers on his desk, signing off the pay sheets and the monthly account for the agistment of the twelve horses that belonged to the sheriff's office. But his eyes kept glancing back to the upright envelope with the telegraph.

When he finally picked it up, it was with a feeling of concern. Before Joseph Bunny's arrival in Eureka Falls the day before with the body of Victor Kerry, life for Sheriff Will Price had been uncomplicated. The town was prosperous, well run by the mayor and town council, and a model of law and order. The result of the latest census now advised that Eureka Falls had 408 permanent citizens and that it was growing moderately, but nevertheless, growing.

'We are now over four hundred inhabitants, Will,' had said Mayor Foy with pride. 'On our way to becoming a fully fledged city.'

Will knew that the mayor saw people as voters, while it was the sheriff and his three deputies who had to ensure that all those good citizens remained law abiding. Not that Will saw any great difficulty with doing that. The 408 citizens of Eureka Falls were mostly good and decent folk. Some of the young men tended to get rowdy but that was predictable, expected even — an aspect of youth that, when mixed with booze on a payday, usually ended in a fistfight but not much more. The cell in sheriff's office was hardly ever used; in fact it was now storage space for old furniture. No, if trouble ever came to Eureka Falls it usually came from outside, riding into town to upset the balance of life, or 'the equilibrium,' as Mayor Fritz Foy would say. So the trick was to get that trouble on to a horse and to get it riding out of town.

Will rubbed his chin as he thought, isn't that exactly what Lake City had done? Released Victor Kerry on the condition that he leaves? Trouble was, Lake City had just passed their trouble on to Eureka Falls.

But could this have been avoided? Will held the envelope in his fingers and tapped its edge against the desktop to make the only sound in the office, except for the slow ticking of the pendulum wall clock. What if Joseph

Bunny had buried Victor Kerry in the hills, thought Will? Up on one of the ridges amongst the firs and then returned home to his farm? Even if Kerry was reported missing, who, apart from Carlson, would be interested in searching for him? And as the months went by and turned into a year, well, it would be mostly speculation as to what happened. Maybe, he fell from his horse to die a lonely death in a remote valley? Or drowned while crossing a swollen creek? Or maybe a fall at night down a deserted mine shaft? Or frozen to death by early snow? But no, Joseph Bunny had killed a man and bought his body to Eureka Falls as a good law-abiding citizen.

'Pity he didn't take him back to Wes Nettleton,' mumbled Will. 'This is really your problem, Wes, not mine.'

But it was Will's problem. Joseph Bunny, the honest but sometimes abrupt farmer, had confessed to murder and was happy to be arrested. But why? Did he wish to relieve his conscience?

That didn't seem likely. He showed no remorse for killing Kerry or for the way he had done it. 'So why turn yourself in?' mulled the sheriff. It made no sense.

Will sat in silence, deep in thought, tapped the envelope up and down in time with the ticking of the large wall clock. Tap, tic, tap, tic, tap, tic. But it was the situation with Carlson that worried the sheriff the most. If he and his associates rode hard, they would be in Eureka Falls tomorrow and there was no doubt that they would want to confront Joseph Bunny. Or, thought Will, maybe Joseph Bunny will want to confront them. After all the man seemed to know no fear, he'd shown that by chasing down Victor Kerry. But Will had taken from Bunny his handgun, rifle, and the Schofield revolver that had belonged to Victor Kerry, which left him with no more than a rope and knife, and that would be no help against Carlson and any hired guns he might have with him.

The sheriff picked up the envelope and took out the telegraph.

To the Sheriff of Eureka Falls
From the Sheriff of Lake City
Black Jack Carlson left with seven associates, including Gavin Bryant, Len Marlow and the Patterson brothers, Bill and Sonny. Expect they will arrive at Eureka Falls Wednesday or Thursday. Their intentions are unknown but I urge caution.
Wes Nettleton

'Eight all up. The Patterson brothers,' said Will out loud. He knew of the Pattersons from the gazettes. They were two killers who had been in and out of the State Penitentiary, but had both managed to avoid the noose through luck and luck alone.

The office door opened to the chatter of his three deputies as they entered. 'You need us anymore, Sheriff?' asked Lonny.

'Yes, I do, Lon, I want you boys to clean out our cell.'

'Now?'

'Yep, right now.'

'Who are you going to put in there, Sheriff?' asked Deputy Edward Taft, the youngest of the three.

'Joseph Bunny,' said the sheriff.

'You going to arrest him for the murder of Victor Kerry?' asked Deputy Pendle Doogan.

'No. I'm going to arrest him for his own protection.'

10

The Mayor

Wednesday 5 June 1878 — Morning

Joseph Bunny made his bed, folding the two blankets neatly and placing them to the end of the low metal cot, before perching himself upon a small stool to begin waxing his boots. The cell door was unlocked and ajar and he looked up as Sheriff Will Price pushed it open.

'Do you like beans, Mr Bunny?'

'Joseph,' responded Bunny.

'Joseph,' repeated the sheriff.

'Are you cooking?' asked Bunny.

'No, it comes from the boarding-house where you were staying. Only this time I'm paying for it.'

'That seems like a fine arrangement.' The brush strokes on the boot were vigorous. 'If you give me your boots, I'll return the favour.'

'It is no favour you are under protection.' The sheriff paused then added, 'Joseph.'

Joseph chuckled. 'Seems like a favour to me, you wanting to watch over me and then feed me free of charge, especially seeing I have confessed to murder. What I don't figure is why you still haven't arrested me.'

'Well, I have detained you under the provisions of the law that says you are assisting with my investigations.'

Bunny picked up the other boot and began to rub wax into the toe. 'Had I known Eureka Falls was so friendly I would have packed up and moved here.'

'Really?' was the sheriff's response.

'No, probably not. Lin and I got lucky when we took up land in the valley and it was all I ever wanted.'

'So who is looking after it while you are away? A neighbour?'

'No, I turned out the stock and opened the gates where there's plenty of feed, mainly in the top paddocks where the creek flows all year. They'll be fine for a week or two but I wouldn't want to leave it too long though. Farming on your own means there are not enough hours in the day for all the things that need to be done. So there will be plenty to do when I get back.' Bunny didn't look up as he spoke; he was busy rubbing wax into the side of the boot so he didn't get to see the look of enquiry in the sheriff's eyes.

'You have no wife, Joseph?'

'No, my brother won that prize, not me.'

'And your brother's place? Who's looking after that?'

'Heather's place,' Bunny corrected. 'Did the same. We share fences and gates but yes there will be more for me to do now, so I will probably have to sell, unless I can get free of Carlson some other way.'

'So, back in a week or two?' said the sheriff.

'Yes,' said Bunny without lifting his head, intent on the job of brushing his boots to a fine sheen. 'And if you want those boots cleaned up, just pull them off and leave them here before I put the lid back on this tin of wax.'

The sheriff was still thinking of what Bunny had said when he walked up to the mayor's office. Joseph had turned out the stock then taken off after Victor Kerry with a mind to kill him and return in a week or two. Then why the hell did he turn himself in? And why did he seem to want to be charged for the murder? When Will had told Bunny that he wanted to hold him in custody, he agreed willingly and packed up his belongings to walk over to the sheriff's office from the boarding-house. In fact, he helped the deputies clean out the last of the furniture from the cell and mop the floor. When Will had asked for a gentleman's agreement that he not leave the building, Bunny had given it freely but added, 'If you need to lock me up, then go ahead, Sheriff.'

The sheriff was still considering these

matters when he arrived at the mayor's office.

Mayor Fritz Foy had come to Eureka Falls as a young man to prospect but had little luck in finding any precious metals. His success was in the organizing of his fellow miners in the itinerant camp that was to become the town he now presided over. His name was Fritz Foyenberg then, which he changed to Fred Foy when first seeking election as a town councillor, but everybody still called him Fritz and so it just stuck.

Fritz loved everything that came with being the Mayor of Eureka Falls, but especially he loved the mayoral chain and wore it at every opportunity. It was a polished metal affair that hung around his large neck, below his second chin. Fritz was wearing it when Will met him in the end room of the council chambers.

'Official function?' the sheriff had asked on seeing the chain.

'For a photograph,' replied the mayor with a wide smile. 'A photographer from Chicago is travelling West and recording the life and times in towns like Eureka Falls.' Then Fritz leaned forward close to Will. 'He was most interested when he heard about the body in the blanket outside your office but by the time he got down there with his camera, your deputies had loaded it into Cyril's hearse.' The mayor looked down and straightened the chain around his neck, turning his two chins into three. 'He went and asked Cyril if he could photograph the body, but he refused to let him.'

'I should think so,' said Will. 'It is the body of a deceased man not an animal.'

'Yes, but a murdered deceased man, I believe,' said the mayor.

'His name is Victor Kerry and, yes, it would seem so,' said Will.

'Only seem?'

'The man who brought the body into Eureka Falls is named Joseph Bunny, from over near Lake City. He is known to Sheriff Wes Nettleton who has vouched for him. Bunny says he killed

Victor Kerry in retribution for the rape and murder of his sister-in-law on Tuesday of last week.'

The mayor shook his head. 'I heard. A terrible business,' he said. 'What is Lake City turning into?'

The sheriff let the remark pass, at least for now. 'Bunny has admitted to me that he tracked, caught and cut off Victor Kerry's appendage, before he bled to death.'

'Appendage? You mean? Oh!' The mayor looked a little pale. 'Where is this man Joseph Bunny now?'

'In our cell.'

'Thank God for that, he sounds like a madman.'

'Mad? I don't know.' Will tapped a finger against his chin. 'Victor Kerry was a giant of a man, called Moose, which I'm sure relates to his size. To take him on was no mean feat. Wes Nettleton believes that Kerry was responsible for the death of Heather Bunny, so my sympathies lie with Joseph Bunny, not with Victor Kerry.'

'Ah, but that is not for you to decide, Will. That must be left to the courts. You have done right by arresting him for murder, but his fate will be with the circuit judge who will be here next month.'

'Who said I have arrested him for murder?'

The mayor's brow furrowed. 'This man, Bunny, has admitted to the murder, so of course you must arrest him. You said he is in your cell.'

'That's right, for protection.'

'Whose protection?'

'For his protection, as I believe he may be in danger. Danger from a man and his associates from over Cheyenne Wells way, who, I now know, also has extensive business interests in Lake City.'

'Who is that?'

'The employer of Victor Kerry, a Mr Black Jack Carlson.'

The mayor went to speak, but although his mouth opened and closed, nothing came out. His fingers touched at the mayoral chain nervously as a faint sound came from his lips.

'Sorry, Mayor?' said Will. 'Did you say something?'

The mayor coughed. 'Jack Carlson,' he said, his voice pitched high.

'You know him?'

'I've heard,' said the mayor, but he sounded evasive.

'Travelling with Carlson are seven other men and two of them are the Patterson brothers, Bill and Sonny. Both are killers. Wes Nettleton, over at Lake, says they are on their way and I figure they will be here either later today or early tomorrow.' The mayor shuffled on the spot uncomfortably as the sheriff spoke. 'Wes says that he is unsure of Carlson's intentions but urges caution. At first I thought Carlson might just wish to claim the body and take it back to Cheyenne Wells but you don't need to bring seven men to do that and you don't need the likes of the Patterson brothers.'

'So you think . . . ' Small beads of

sweat had appeared on the mayor's top lip.

'I think they are coming for Joseph Bunny.'

The mayor licked his top of lip, leaving it moist and shiny. 'This is most alarming, most alarming. What are you going to do?'

'I'm going to protect Bunny until such time as I decide what he should be charged with. At the moment I don't know if it should be murder, torture, bravery or doing public good. But it's what I want you to do, Mr Mayor.'

Fritz was now decidedly nervous. 'Me? What can I do?'

'You can meet Jack Carlson with me when he arrives and advise him that it isn't just the sheriff protecting Joseph Bunny from harm, but all of Eureka Falls. Because unless I have the backing from this town, me and my three deputies are going to be outnumbered. And four against eight isn't going to work if they want to forcibly take Bunny and lynch him.'

'We can't have that, it would be, be ... ' The mayor seemed to be searching for the words.

'Unlawful?' said the sheriff.

'Bad,' said the mayor. 'Very bad for the name of Eureka Falls.'

Sheriff Will Price shook his head. 'Bad?' he repeated. 'Bad for the name of Eureka Falls? I can't see it being much better for Joseph Bunny either.'

But the sheriff's observation seemed to be lost on the mayor who was nervously straightening the chain around his neck.

11

The Alamo

Wednesday 5 June 1878 — Early Afternoon

'Lonny, I want all the furniture you took from the cell moved to the front of the office and stacked, neat, so that when you've done it this place doesn't look like the Alamo.'

Lonny had been nodding his head vigorously but now he was shaking it slowly, clearly confused at what Will wanted.

Will placed a hand on Lonny's shoulder. 'Just get on with it and then I'll take a look. And later, I want you to clean every gun we own, just in case we need them.'

'Sure, Sheriff.' Lonny's words didn't mask his concern.

Will walked to the back of the office and down the hall to the cell. He checked the large iron bolt on the back door then looked at the furniture stacked against the side wall. He was deep in thought when Joseph Bunny spoke from behind the iron bars of the cage, where he was stitching the edge of a frayed pocket on a well-worn shirt.

'If you want to give me your boots I'll have them looking pretty for you.'

'Not now, Joseph.'

'Well, that's an improvement.'

'What was that?' Will's voice was matter-of-fact and a little brusque.

'You called me Joseph. I said that was an improvement over being called Mr Bunny.'

'Yes, so I did.' The sheriff's voice softened.

'I could hear what you were saying to your deputy, but no matter how you make it look, if you stack that furniture up front, this place is still going to look like the Alamo.'

'You got any better suggestions?'

asked the sheriff.

'Yep, if you build a fortress you'll be forced to defend it. If you can get every man in this town to shoot these dogs as soon as they ride in, then it's all over and done with.'

'I'm not too sure I should do that; I'm the sheriff and supposed to protect this town, not get the good citizens into a war. Besides, I'm not to sure if this is really their fight.'

'Well, a war is what you are going to get once Carlson arrives, and wars are a little hard to keep corralled.'

'There'll be no war if I can help it.'

'But can you help it? Do you really know what you are up against?'

'I've seen some, over the years, so I think I know what I'm up against.'

'I guess you are talking about your time in the army.' Bunny stopped to rethread the needle. 'Wes Nettleton has told me about you. He says you are a brave man. Says you fought at Frederickburg and Shenandoah Valley with distinction.'

Will shrugged without making comment.

'Me,' said Bunny, 'me and my brother got to see war at Cumberland and Tullahoma.' He continued to stitch, looking down, intent on the task at hand. 'Real nasty business and if I think about it I can't sleep, so I don't think about it. But our war, yours and mine, was against an honourable opponent. Black Jack Carlson is not an honourable man and if he wants to lynch me, then the only way you're going to stop him is by killing him. Trouble is, when he gets here it will be with reinforcements. He always travels with reinforcements, lots of reinforcements.'

'So I hear,' said Will.

'So you know who he's bringing with him?'

'I've got an idea.'

'You want to share that with me?'

Will thought for a moment. 'He's bringing seven, which includes the Patterson brothers.'

Bunny smiled. 'Seven, ah, with the Patterson brothers included. Carlson is serious, isn't he? That will be you and your three deputies against eight. I think you better give me back my guns to even up the odds a little for the shoot out.'

'I don't think it will come to that.'

'Yeah? Moving furniture to barricade the front of this building seems to say different.'

'I've spoken to the mayor and I've asked him to speak with Carlson as soon as he arrives.'

'Well, I hope he has more steel in his spine than the Mayor of Lake City.'

Will didn't answer.

'Mmm,' said Bunny at Will's silence. 'That doesn't sound good. And what is the Mayor of Eureka Falls going to tell Mr Black Jack Carlson?'

'That this town is behind the law,' said Will, with a hint of defiance.

'But I thought you said you weren't sure if this is really their fight. So is it true? Is the town really behind you?'

'This is a peaceful town of good, law-abiding citizens and it doesn't tolerate lawlessness.'

'Sounds just like Lake City, but this isn't about being peaceful and law-abiding citizens, it's about standing up for what is right. When the sheriff at Lake let Victor Kerry go, on orders from the mayor, the peaceful and law-abiding citizens of Lake City didn't just tolerate it, they breathed a sigh of relief. Sure they were sympathetic to what had happened. A woman raped and murdered is a nasty business, but they didn't want to get involved. Peaceful people want a peaceful life, even if that peace doesn't extend to their neighbour.' Joseph Bunny leant forward and bit the thread of the cotton to break it. 'Had I not gone after Victor Kerry, then no one would have. Not the law, and certainly not the politicians, like our mayor, and not our peaceful citizens. The way I see it, I had no choice, I had to do what needed to be done.' Bunny pinned the needle into the cuff of his shirt for safe keeping while he inspected his handiwork. 'And I guess you think the same because you still haven't arrested me for the murder of Victor Kerry. I know you accept that I killed him but you must feel that it was justified.' Bunny withdrew the needle and held it to the light and rethreaded it. 'Truth be, I thought I was going to die trying to do it, but I figured that was better than living and having done nothing. I wouldn't have been able to sleep because it would always be on my mind what Kerry had done to our Heather. She'd come and visit me in my dreams, asking if anyone cared what had happened to her.'

Will touched his chin, then self-consciously let his hand drop back to his side.

'You sure you don't want to give me your boots? I'll have them looking like new for you.' Joseph smiled as he looked at the sheriff.

Will turned to go, deep in thought. 'Not now Joseph, not now.'

12

The Buffalo Gun

Wednesday 5 June 1878 — Late Afternoon

'Lonny, I can give you a hand if you want.'

'I don't know if that would be a good idea, you cleaning our guns and being in jail.'

'Well I may be in jail but I'm here because the sheriff wants to protect me, and I agreed to it. That's why he left the cell door unlocked, but I've got two spare hands and you've got a lot of guns to clean.'

Lonny looked up at the rifle cabinet with its row of Winchesters standing upright. 'I have.'

'Well if you want to put these hands to work, I'm here.'

Deputy Sheriff Lonny Pitkin looked at Joseph Bunny sitting on the small stool in his cell with his legs stretched out as he rubbed his right knee. Lonny then looked back up at the rifle cabinet.

'All you need to do is check the weapon is unloaded then hand it to me,' said Bunny. 'Then you just need to give me a cleaning cloth, oil and a brush and we'll get the job done in half the time.'

Lonny looked back up at the gun cabinet.

'Give me something to do and stop me from being idle. I hate being idle. Not good for a man to be idle,' added Joseph Bunny.

Lonny wiped the cloth down the length of the Winchester barrel with his eyes still on the rifle cabinet.

'Did I do a fine job on your boots?'

Lonny looked down at his freshly waxed boots. 'Yes you did, I can't deny that; they look as good as new.'

'I can do the same with the rifles.'

Lonny relented. 'Just one at a time and you are to stay in the cell.'

'I can only clean one at a time and I ain't going anywhere.'

Lonny went to the rifle cabinet and selected the next Winchester to be cleaned. He pulled the lever down then up, repeating the action several times, then looked into the chamber and magazine to check that it was unloaded. He walked back and handed it over.

'Now I need some of that cloth and oil. And one of the brushes you've got over there.'

Lonny collected the items and returned to the cell. Bunny had pulled down the lever action and pushed his thumb into the chamber so that the light reflected off his thumbnail as he looking down the barrel. 'I think there might be a spider living down there.'

'Wouldn't be surprised,' said Lonny. 'Some of these rifles haven't been fired for years.'

'No need to ever arm up a posse then?'

'No, never had any of that sort of trouble since I've been a deputy.' Lonny walked across to a tall cabinet, unlocked the door and drew out a long firearm.

'What's that?' asked Bunny as he looked up from cleaning the Winchester on his lap.

'Sharps rifle.'

'What's it used for? Elephants?'

'Buffalo mostly.'

'And the tube on top?'

'Optical sight so you can shoot straight at a very long range.'

'How long?'

'Thousand yards, so they say.'

'That's long. What do you boys use it for?'

'Well, nothing really, not yet at least. The sheriff used one similar in the war, but this one was recovered when an old buffalo hunter shot himself out near Western Creek.'

'Deliberate?'

'Yes, sir, under the chin. He used his toe on the trigger.'

'Big gun like that would make a terrible mess.'

'Point five two, and it did. The sheriff said we should keep the rifle, just in case we need to shoot over a long distance.'

'You fired it?'

'Yes, the sheriff showed us how, but we couldn't shoot as straight as him.'

'So he's a straight shooter?'

'Yes, sir, he's a real sharpshooter.'

'Does it take paper or metallic cartridges?'

'Metallic.'

'So it can shoot fast.'

'Sheriff shot ten rounds into a target at three hundred yards in less than one minute and hit the bull's eye nine times out of ten.'

'Now that I'd like to see,' said Joseph as he looked back down the Winchester's barrel to check that it was clean. 'You should call your sheriff, Buffalo Will.'

Lonny laughed out loud. 'Yes, sir, Sheriff Buffalo Will Price. I like that,' he said, as he cleaned the long barrel of the Sharps rifle.

13

A Pleasant Stay

Wednesday 5 June 1878 — Evening

The riders came out of the evening gloom at the top end of Main Street, three abreast, walking their horses easy. Black Jack Carlson was in the middle, sitting tall. Behind him were three more riders who were then followed by a buckboard with two more men.

Deputy Sheriffs Pendle Doogan and Edward Taft had seen them first from a distance and doubled back on foot to tell the sheriff. Will Price dispatched Ed with haste to get the mayor and told Doogan to get Lonny, quick. When Lon arrived he told him and Doogan to lock Joseph Bunny in the cell and to arm themselves, each with a loaded Winchester.

'Loaded? Inside? In the office?' asked Pendle Doogan, who knew that it was a standing order to keep the rifles unloaded when in the office.

Will nodded. 'Yes, loaded in the office, to protect Mr Bunny.'

Will walked across the street to meet the mayor with the greeting, 'Time to become acquainted with Black Jack Carlson.'

The mayor coughed nervously, hesitating before he followed behind Will, taking small timid steps. Carlson and his men had stopped outside the saloon and started to dismount. When he saw the sheriff, Carlson raised his arm to signal to the others to stop talking.

'Looks like you were expecting us.' Carlson's voice was strong and confident.

'Lake City sheriff notified me,' said Will. 'I believe you're here to collect the body of Victor Kerry.'

'We are, Sheriff. And I believe you have the man who killed him.'

'I have. He is in custody.'

'And I believe that man is Joseph Bunny.'

'That is correct,' answered Will.

'His brother's wife was killed last week.' Carlson turned his head as he spoke and looked around, as if casting an eye over the town.

'So I understand,' said Will, keeping his gaze fixed on Carlson. 'I also understand that she was attacked and killed by Victor Kerry.'

Carlson continued to look around. 'That has not been proven and now with the death of Moose, well, I guess it never will be.'

Will let Carlson's comment pass. 'So, you plan on heading back tomorrow?'

'Sheriff, we have just arrived after a hard ride. My men would like to rest and take some refreshment.' Carlson's hand waved to the entrance of the saloon.

'Yes, I've noticed your men.' Will cast his eyes towards the group of riders and the two men who still remained seated on the buckboard. 'Eight of you to pick up a body? That could be seen as, well, unnecessary.'

'I couldn't stop them, Sheriff. They have all come as a sign of respect.'

'I see,' said Will. 'Respect.' But his tone came out with a hint of mocking as he turned his head towards Fritz. 'The mayor would like to say a few words. Mayor?'

The mayor coughed nervously. 'Mr Carlson, this is a most regrettable situation, a man being killed and the circumstances.'

Will felt the muscles in his back tighten and a nagging soreness from years in the saddle stab down low on the left side, along with a voice in his head that shouted. Jeezus, Fritz, shut up about the circumstances and get on with it.

'But I want to let you know, Mr Carlson, that this town stands for law and order.'

'I would hope so,' said Carlson. 'You have the man who murdered one of my men in jail, so I expect law and order to be carried out.'

The mayor went to speak but Will cut him short. 'It is yet to be proved who killed Victor Kerry.'

'But I hear he has admitted it.'

The mayor went to speak again but Will answered first. 'Admitted but not yet proved.'

Carlson scowled as the mayor puffed-up his girth before he spoke. 'May I welcome you and your men to Eureka Falls and may I hope that you have a pleasant stay.'

Oh shit, Fritz, thought Will. Welcome? A pleasant stay? What are you doing? We are not a welcoming committee. We are here to enforce law and order against a lynching party of eight armed men.

14

Cut How?

Thursday 6 June 1878 — Morning

The tail of the buckboard nudged up
with a jolt against the landing at the
back of John W. Wilks & Son. Cyril
Wilks stood at the back door watching,
his heels together as if standing to
attention in a sign of respect. When
Carlson walked towards him, Cyril
extended his hand in a sombre gesture.

'Mr Carlson, if you come through to
my office we can complete the release
of the body of Mr Victor Kerry.'

Carlson nodded his silent agreement
and followed the undertaker into the
large dim room. In the centre was the
silhouette of an oversized coffin on
three wooden trestles, lit by the yellow
glow of an oil lamp.

'It will take six of your men to lift the coffin,' said Cyril.

'Can they do that now?' asked Carlson.'

'Not until the body has been released from my care,' said Cyril. 'Once I have your signature that you have accepted the mortal remains of Mr Kerry, then your men can load. But not before then. It is the law.'

Carlson nodded again as he passed the large casket and entered the undertaker's office, close behind Cyril.

'The documents require your full name, address, date and signature. In signing, you accept responsibility as the employer, for the body, in the absence of any known kin.' The undertaker's words were businesslike.

'I understand,' said Carlson in a firm, clear voice.

'Please, sit and use my desk, Mr Carlson.' Cyril turned his hand over in a slow wave.

Jack Carlson sat, looked over the documents then started to complete the form. 'And the death certificate?' he asked, as he wrote.

'A copy of the certificate of death is attached at the back of the documents. It was raised by our town physician, Dr Mervan Larson.'

'And cause of death?' asked Carlson.

Cyril remained quiet and glanced at the floor.

'Cause of death?' Carlson asked again.

'It is on the certificate.' The undertaker's eyes kept looking at the floor.

Carlson flicked through the papers to the last page. He read in silence before he looked up and fixed his gaze on Cyril. 'Says he bled to death.'

'That's right,' said the undertaker nervously.

'Shot, then bled to death?'

'No.'

'Then how?'

'Cut.'

'Cut how?'

'With a knife.'

Carlson slapped his hand on the

desk, the sharp crack cutting through the stillness of the dim room. 'Of course with a knife, but *how* was he cut? Was he stabbed? And if so, how many times?'

Cyril restlessly shifted his weight from one foot to the other and started to stammer. 'No, no, no, not stabbed, just cut, resulting in a large loss of blood.'

'And where precisely was that cut?'

'To the lower regions.'

'The lower regions?' Carlson's look was piercing. 'Precisely where in the lower regions?'

Cyril's mouth opened but there were no words for a second or two, before he finally said. 'The genitals.'

'What?' The shout filled the office. 'The genitals? How were his genitals cut?'

Cyril coughed as he tried to regain composure. 'Removed,' he said in a low voice.

'What was that, Mr Undertaker?'

'His genitals were completely removed.'

Carlson leaped to his feet, the chair

falling back to bang on the floor then roll on its side.

'First I want you to show me exactly what was done to Moose and then I want you to get the mayor and the sheriff, right here, immediately.'

15

Friends

Thursday 6 June 1878 — Mid Morning

The mayor's face was flushed and he seemed to be puffing like a steam engine with small breaths, while Black Jack Carlson stood tall and motionless, his eyes filled with anger.

'What sort of animal would do that?' he spat.

The mayor's eyes now showed fright and his mouth opened and closed between puffs. 'I, I, I . . . '

Carlson dismissed the mayor with a glance then looked at Will. 'Are you able to explain, Sheriff?'

'Do I need to?'

'Damn right you do, you are holding the man who did it.'

'That is yet to be proved, before we

even look at the reasons why.' The sheriff leant a little forward, a sign that he wasn't going to be intimidated by Carlson.

Carlson also leant forward. 'Nothing could justify what has been done to Vic. It was a savage act.'

'So is the rape and murder of a defenceless woman.' Will's voice was calm but his stance showed that his body was balanced and ready to react.

Carlson seemed to ignore the sheriff's words as he set his glare back on the mayor. 'Joseph Bunny should be handed over to me, to escort back to Lake City.'

The mayor went to speak but Will spoke first. 'For what purpose?'

'So he can go to trial in the town in which he is a citizen.'

'He can go to trial here.' Then Will added, 'If necessary.' The words seemed to rile Carlson.

'Eureka Falls is a small town.' Carlson had now raised his voice. 'You have to wait until the circuit judge comes from Lake and that'll take over a month. I can have Bunny back in two days, three at the most. He can then be tried next week.'

The mayor seemed to seize on the proposal. 'I can see merit in that,' he said.

'Well, I don't,' said Will. 'There is no need for haste to take this to court, when I am yet to finish my investigation. And' — he paused and looked at the mayor — 'transportation of a prisoner can only be done by an officer of the law.'

'Well, give me one of your deputies,' said Carlson. 'You have three. That seems more than enough for a town this size.'

'I have three deputies because they work shifts. One is on duty in the office, one tours the town and the outskirts, and one is on rest.'

'But,' said the mayor. 'Under the circumstances — '

'No,' said Will, the word sharp and abrupt. 'I am not losing a deputy for six days to take a prisoner to Lake then return when there is no need.'

Carlson looked at Will. 'Do you know who you are dealing with, Sheriff?' The words were laced with menace.

Will stayed calm. 'I have an idea.'

'I have friends in positions of influence in Lake City and Cheyenne Wells.'

'That you may, Mr Carlson, but this isn't Cheyenne Wells or Lake City. It's Eureka Falls and your influence doesn't extend this far.'

'Not yet,' said Black Jack Carlson. 'But it will, I'll make sure of it.'

16

Only Shame

Thursday 6 June 1878 — Noon

'I'm keeping you locked up, Joseph.'

Joseph didn't even look up from the boots he was waxing. 'I'm not going anywhere, so it matters little if the cell door is locked or open. Being stuck in an iron cage isn't like being locked in a closet. I can still talk to your deputies and if I sit in the corner, I can see right through to your front door. Could say it's a room with a view.'

The sheriff was in his socks as he closed the door and turned the key. 'One of my deputies or myself will sit back here and keep you company.'

Lonny walked down the narrow hall, a Winchester in his hand, the barrel pointing to the ceiling.

'Armed company,' said Bunny as he brushed up a sheen on one of the sheriff's boots. 'So Black Jack Carlson is in town?'

'Yes,' said the sheriff.

'Patterson brothers?'

'Yep.'

'Anyone else I may know?'

Will returned to his desk and picked up the note he had received from the boarding-house, listing the names from the register. He returned and read them aloud to Joseph. 'Bryant, Marlow, Barrett, Hart and Brooks.'

'I know of some of them. Hired guns out of Cheyenne Wells, so it sounds like a lynching party, doesn't it?'

'Not if I can help it.'

'Me, too,' said Bunny but his voice showed no fear, it was said as easy and as matter-of-fact as someone passing the time of day.

★　★　★

When Will caught up with the mayor it was just after midday and by then the sheriff's office had been barricaded-up with two deputies now on twenty-four hour duty. One sat in the front office with the other next to the cell and both were armed with loaded rifles. It was the chambering of a metallic cartridge into the breech of the rifle that bought home to the deputies the seriousness of the situation. Rifles were always unloaded on the veranda, with the muzzle pointed upright before entering the office. Even handguns had to be carried with one empty chamber, the one over which the hammer was placed forward.

'If someone comes in to take Joseph,' asked Lonny, 'Do I shoot them?'

'Not straight away, Lonny,' said Will with a dry touch of humour. 'But I want to make it clear to the three of you, we protect those in our care with our lives. It comes with the star on your chest.' The three faces all looked concerned. 'That's why few people can do this job, but I know you three boys can and I know that you can do it well.' A little relief came back to their faces. 'Now I'll be here with you and together we will work through this, nice and easy. OK?'

When he got their response it was with renewed enthusiasm and Will felt a sense of pride in his three young deputies, as he reflected on their keenness while walking to the mayor's office.

'This is most serious,' said the mayor. 'It really has nothing to do with us, not Eureka Falls, this is Lake City business.'

'Not now,' was Will's response.

'But if Bunny was to be returned to Lake City to stand trial then it would be best for all.'

'For all?' mocked Will.

'Mr Carlson came and saw me here in my office and put forward a proposal.'

'Oh yeah, and what proposal was that?'

'He said I had the authority to make one of his men a temporary deputy for the transportation of Bunny back to Lake City.'

Will couldn't believe what he was hearing and he didn't know if he should spit, yell or thump the mayor. He clenched his fists and drew in a breath as he silently called on his long dead grandfather to give him guidance from above.

'What did you say?' asked Will.

'I said no.'

Thank God for that, thought Will.

'But . . .'

But what, thought Will?

'But Carlson said if I didn't he could get the mayor from Lake City to give him the authority he needed.'

Will shook his head. 'And how is he planning on doing that?'

'Telegraph.'

The word struck like a fist in Will's ribs.

The mayor looked up. 'Regrettable, regrettable,' he said.

'Regrettable? Regrettable? What does that mean?'

'Well,' said Fritz, 'if the mayor of Lake authorizes one of his men to be temporary deputy then we have no choice but to let Jack Carlson take Bunny back to Lake City.'

'And do you think Joseph Bunny would make it back to Lake City alive?'

The mayor shrugged his shoulders.

'Fritz, this is a man's life — a farmer from just the other side of the pass who came to us for help.'

'I don't think so, Will. He killed a man and he brought the body to us, that's all.'

'That's not all, Fritz. Joseph Bunny bought the body here because Lake City and Cheyenne Wells are towns owned by Black Jack Carlson. He came here looking for justice and he's willing to die for it, that I am sure. He's come here for help and to make a stand.'

Fritz's cheeks were crimson and he was making small puffing sounds. 'But — '

'But nothing, this is the time for Eureka Falls to stand up. If we don't, Carlson will never leave us alone.'

'No, Will,' The mayor was shaking his head. 'I'm certain that Carlson has no interest in Eureka Falls and although it is regrettable for the mayor of Lake to intervene on our behalf, it could be for the better.'

'The better? The better? If we fail this test, there will be no *better* for Eureka Falls, only shame.'

17

The Telegraph

Thursday 6 June 1878 — Afternoon

Will saw the look of concern on Aubin Mead's face as he entered the telegraph office.

'Yes, Carlson has been in to send a telegraph,' answered the clerk, who then turned away from Will.

'You want to show me what it said?'

Aubin now seemed nervous. 'I don't know if I should,' he called over his shoulder. 'It's like mail, it shouldn't just be read by anyone.'

'I'm not anyone, Aubin, I'm the sheriff.'

'So this is official?'

'As official as it can get.'

'I'll need your signature to say so,' said Aubin, his voice shaky.

'And precisely what do you want me to sign?'

'Well, I don't rightly know, but if Mr Carlson was to learn that a personal telegraph of his was read by another party . . . '

'Another party? Personal telegraph?' Will had had enough. 'This is horseshit, Aubin. Our mayor has told me that Carlson has telegraphed the mayor of Lake City, seeking authority to have one of his men made a temporary deputy for the transportation of Joseph Bunny back to Lake City. Now is that correct?'

The telegraph clerk seemed to have taken fright and was now standing well back from the counter. 'Yes, yes, that's right.' The words were fractured. 'And it could be for the best. The people of this town don't want to get involved in this business.'

Will ignored what he had just heard. 'Give me a look at the telegraph before I have to take it by force.'

Aubin turned and quickly shuffled

across to the wall and pulled a telegraph form from one of the pigeon holes then returned to Will.

'When was it sent?' asked Will.

'Just over an hour ago.'

The sheriff read the telegraph, which was marked urgent. It was chilling in its simplicity. It directed that a return telegraph be sent immediately with the following text:

I, as Mayor of Lake City, do hereby authorise Harris Brooks to be Deputy Sheriff for the transfer of Joseph Bunny from Eureka Falls to Lake City forthwith, for the purpose of standing trial for the murder of Victor Kerry.

'Was Carlson here with anyone?'

'Three men.'

'Was one of them Brooks?'

'I believe so.' Aubin had stepped back again from the counter as Will questioned him.

'Do you know why he chose Brooks?'

'I believe he is the only one of Mr Carlson's associates who has not been in jail. Seems the others could be excluded from holding a deputy's appointment if they have a criminal conviction.'

'He told you that?'

'Not me, but I heard them. They were talking and sorting it out.'

'I see,' said Will, as he continued to examine the telegraph. 'What time do you close, Aubin?'

The telegraph clerk glanced at the clock on the wall. 'In forty-three minutes. Right on five.'

'I want you to close now.'

'But if I close now, Mr Carlson won't get his return telegraph from the mayor of Lake City.'

'That's why I want you to close up, now. He can have his return telegraph tomorrow morning, first thing, but not today.'

'But, Sheriff, I can't do what you're asking me — '

'But I'm not asking, Aubin,' interrupted Will. 'As the sheriff of this town

I'm ordering you to close the Eureka Falls telegraph office now.'

Aubin looked around nervously, just as the dit-dash sounds of the Morse code signalled an incoming telegraph.

'I should answer that,' said the telegraph clerk. 'It's Lake City.'

The clicking of the key repeated and Aubin turned, then glanced back, just as Sheriff Will Price's right hand fell to the grip of his Army Colt.

Aubin Mead saw the movement and sucked in a sharp breath. 'What will I tell Mr Carlson? He is expecting a return telegraph today.'

'Don't tell him anything until tomorrow. Close up and walk down to my office with me, then at five, go straight home.'

'Go with you?'

'That's right, down to my office where my deputies are on duty. And,' added the sheriff, 'where you can meet the man whose life you might just have saved.'

The telegraph key clicked again,

calling out down the copper wire from Lake City for a response.

'You're not giving me a choice, are you, Sheriff?'

Will knew what the telegraph clerk was asking. Aubin didn't want to make a choice; he didn't want to make a decision.

'That's right Aubin, it's an order from the Sheriff of Eureka Falls.'

18

Defend Your Town

Thursday 6 June 1878 — Just Before Midnight

Lonny walked the two horses from the stables, down the lane in the dark and to the back of the sheriff's office. One of the horses was saddled, a coiled rope and two full water canteens hanging from the side, while the other horse, a grey, carried a homemade canvas harness consisting of large green bags that straddled a dark-blue horse blanket. Each canvas bag bulged with supplies of flour, sugar, dried meat, some potatoes, corn, pumpkin and coffee. Separated from the stores were five additional water canteens and, in the smaller pocket with the buckled flap, was flint and dry horsehair to ignite a fire.

Inside, Joseph sat in his cell silently at work as he stitched repairs to one of his boots. He pushed the needle through the edge of the separated sole using a leather pad to protect the palm of his hand, then pulled tight on the coarse white thread to bind the worn layers back together. He worked like a tradesman keeping the stitches small, close and neat.

As the back door opened for Lonny to enter, Joseph heard one of the horses snort and looked up. It was a sound he knew well but why, he thought, had his horse been brought to the rear of the sheriff's office? As he continued to stitch with his head bent forward, he called to the deputy.

'Lonny, what are you doing with my girl?'

Lonny stamped his feet on the straw mat to remove the dust from his polished boots. 'Sheriff got me to get both your horses for you, Mr Bunny, and load them up with supplies.'

Joseph knew what this meant and he shook his head and let the boot fall to the ground. 'And I thought I was going to get some sleep tonight.'

Sheriff Will Price's footsteps signalled his arrival as he walked down the narrow hallway to the back room, the oil lamp showing a glow in the surface of his freshly waxed boots. In his hand he held a large black cell key that jangled against the metal tag with the embossed word: Cell.

'I get the feeling that my tenancy is up,' said Joseph Bunny.

The sheriff didn't respond until after he had opened the cell door. 'Come tomorrow morning, when the telegraph office opens, I won't be able to protect you, Joseph.' The sheriff was having trouble looking Bunny in the eye. 'Carlson has called on the mayor of Lake City to authorize one of his men to be made a temporary deputy for your transfer from Eureka Falls to Lake City.'

'Why don't you just refuse to hand

me over?' asked Bunny.

'Not that easy. Carlson could take you by force and still be within the law, and eight against four aren't good odds.'

The look in Bunny's eyes was one of defiance. 'Arm me up and it will be five against eight. Get some more men and we can make it an even fight. Get more and we can easily rid Colorado of the scourge of Jack Carlson.'

'I can't ask men to do that, and if truth be known . . . ' Will paused, his eyes cast to the cell floor. 'I wouldn't be able to get anyone anyway. This is a town of old miners, mild grocers and farmers.'

'That what I am, Sheriff? I'm just a farmer.'

'No, Joseph, you are more than that, much more. You're a fighter and you've shown us up.'

'Including you, it would seem?' There was a hint of insult in Bunny's voice.

Will lifted his head and looked

Bunny in the eye. 'Yes, including me,' he said.

'So, what do you propose I do?'

'I don't rightly know. But I do know that if I hand you over to Carlson, you'll be dead before tomorrow night.'

'Well if that's the case I can't head back to my property,' said Joseph. 'They will just chase me down and lynch me there.'

'You could head south. Once you cross the border and into the Territories, Carlson won't have any legal right to apprehend, hold or transport you.'

'So he just lynches me in the Territories. Is that it?'

'Then I suggest you keep running south.'

Joseph stood and stepped towards Will. 'If we had just a few more men we could defeat Carlson.'

'We don't have a few more men.'

'OK, so it's five of us against eight; it's better than one against eight, because that's what it will be if you turn me out.'

'I have no choice.'

'You have,' said Bunny, 'but you won't take it.'

The three deputies stood behind the sheriff in silence, watching and listening, each with a Winchester in his hands.

'I'm sorry that it has come to this,' said Will.

'So am I,' said Joseph Bunny. 'I thought Eureka Falls would be different.'

'I guess you did, or you wouldn't have bought the body of Victor Kerry here, would you?'

Bunny seemed to curse under his breath.

'You picked Eureka Falls, didn't you?'

Joseph looked up at the ceiling before he slowly nodded his head.

'You want to tell me why?'

Joseph slowly lowered his gaze to look Will in the eye. 'Yeah, I came here on purpose.' He cursed under his breath again. 'Kerry was heading for

Cheyenne Wells not Eureka Falls when I caught him up. I killed him that same night, not the following day around noon, like I said. He died quickly. I was actually closer to Lake but I couldn't take him there. I needed to find a place where I could take on Carlson and his gang, so I had to ride hard to get Kerry's body here. I figured that you and this town would help me defeat Carlson.' Bunny was now shaking his head. 'But I figured wrong.'

'Yes, I guess you did,' said the sheriff. 'It is not this town's fight.'

Bunny looked up. 'Not yet.'

The sheriff handed the cell keys across to Lonny as he spoke. 'Lonny has loaded your horses with enough supplies to get you well into the Territories.'

'I don't need supplies,' said Bunny. 'What I need are weapons and ammunition, plenty of ammunition. My only chance is to find a place where I can ambush Carlson and his men when they come after me. Some ground

116

where I can hold up and try to pick them off. That's the only way I see of having any chance at all; not by trying to outrun eight men hell bent on stringing me up.'

'You could use Bent Canyon,' said Lonny enthusiastically.

Bunny turned towards Lonny. 'You want to tell me about it, Lonny?'

'Sure. Bent is south from here as you head to the Territories, about a day's ride, maybe a little more. It's got steep sides with a good field of view back up to the north. You'd see anyone coming after you, long before they arrived.'

Bunny looked to the sheriff.

Will nodded. 'Lonny is right; Bent Canyon is suitable for an ambush, but I still think you'd be better off leaving Colorado behind and going to the Territories. The odds are against you, even if you were able to take out three or four, but with eight, eventually they'll overrun you.'

Bunny shifted his gaze back to the deputy. 'You want to show me where it is on the map, Lonny?'

'Yes, sir,' said Lonny. 'I can show you.' Lonny turned and walked back up the narrow corridor, the cold sound of clinking cell keys matching the pace of his boots.

'Sheriff?'

'Yes, Joseph.'

'Can you give me back my weapons as well as Victor Kerry's Schofield?'

'Yes, I can do that.'

'And extra ammunition?'

'Yes, that too.'

'And that Sharps rifle?'

'The Sharps?' The sheriff touched his chin as he thought. 'No, Joseph, I can't give you that but I can give you one of the Winchesters as an extra rifle.'

Bunny's mouth pulled tight then relaxed. 'I'll take what you can give and be grateful for it.'

The sheriff and his three deputies stood motionless as Lonny returned holding a map. 'I'll go with you, Mr Bunny,' he said.

Joseph Bunny grinned. 'Nothing I'd

like better, Lonny, but the sheriff is right. This is not your fight, it's mine.'

Lonny looked hurt, as if he'd been dismissed.

'You like Eureka Falls, Lonny?' asked Bunny.

'My hometown.'

'Would you be prepared to fight for it, if someone came to take it away?'

'You bet I would,' said Lonny, his words fast and keen.

'Good lad. Then best you stay here and defend your town. The people here are going to need you more than I do.'

19

The Threat

Friday 7 June 1878 — Morning

Carlson and his men stood around the buckboard where the large coffin of Victor Kerry lay on the bleached timber tray. Will stood observing from the window of his office as the deputies took the last of the furniture from the front room and moved it back into the cell.

The mayor arrived in short fast steps, his face flushed with exertion as he doffed his hat in reverence to Carlson. Will shook his head in displeasure and while he couldn't hear what was being said, he could guess. Carlson was showing him the telegraph he'd received that morning and, as he spoke, the mayor nodded his head vigorously then held a thick black book high. Carlson nodded and called to a young man, who tied his horse to the wheel of the buckboard and sheepishly joined Carlson and the mayor. Carlson introduced the youth to the mayor then pointed to the door of the sheriff's office. Carlson led the way, followed by the mayor and the youth.

Will remained where he was, still watching out the window as the three entered.

'Sheriff,' said Carlson. 'I've come for Joseph Bunny.'

'Really.' The sheriff's response was flat and toneless.

'I know what you did, Sheriff, closing down the telegraph office, but there'll be no further delay. I've got the authority in my hand. I've come for Joseph Bunny, to escort him back to Lake City and the mayor is here to swear in my man.'

'What assurance do I have that he will arrive in Lake safe and sound?'

'Well,' said Carlson, 'we will do our

best under the guidance of Deputy Sheriff Brooks here. But,' Carlson half grinned, 'accidents sometimes happen.'

Harris Brooks smiled.

'I wouldn't smile if I were you, son,' said Will. 'If you take the oath of office as a Coloradoan Deputy Sheriff, you will be responsible and accountable under the law for the safe protection of those in your care. And that includes prisoners.'

The smile left Brooks's face in an instant and his eyes went to Carlson for reassurance.

'That won't be your problem, Sheriff,' said Carlson. 'Nor the problem of this town.'

As Carlson spoke he placed his hand on the mayor's shoulder. Fritz nodded enthusiastically in response, which sickened Will so he turned his gaze back to the six men waiting outside and watched as they checked their weapons.

'What if I can't give you Bunny?'

'You have no choice: I have the

authority and I have shown it to the mayor.'

'He's right,' said Fritz. 'I've seen the telegraph and it has the authority of the mayor of Lake City to affirm Mr Brooks here as a deputy for the transfer of Joseph Bunny. It's all above board,' added the mayor.

'Lonny,' called the sheriff, 'will you get a star and the oath from the cabinet?'

The sound of a wooden drawer could be heard as it opened and closed, then Lonny walked back slowly to the sheriff and handed him a polished metal star and a small brown card. Will then handed the two items over to the mayor.

'Will you assist?' asked the mayor of Will.

'No,' was the curt reply from the sheriff. 'Me and my deputies want no part of this.'

Fritz seemed to choke.

'Just get on with it,' said Carlson, agitated.

'Now take this Bible and repeat after me.' The mayor's voice was shaky. 'I Harris Brooks, do swear that I will faithfully discharge my duties as a temporary deputy sheriff within the laws of the State of Colorado.'

Brooks stumbled through the pledge and as he did Will looked over at his three deputies, their faces dark with contempt. The mayor then pinned the badge upon Brooks's chest, who stood ill at ease with the Bible still clenched in his hand.

'OK, let's get Bunny and get out of this town,' said Carlson. 'Where is he?' He was looking down towards the back of the office to where the corridor led to the cell.

Will looked up at the pendulum clock on the wall. 'I expect that Joseph Bunny is well on his way to Willow Springs by now.'

Carlson continued to look towards the rear of the office. 'What are you talking about? Willow Springs?'

'Willow Springs is south side of the

border, in the Territories, and the authority of your new deputy ends at the border. It's where Colorado law stops.' Will fixed his gaze on Carlson. 'I released Joseph Bunny last night and that's where he is heading.'

The look in Carlson's eyes was a mixture of anger and menace. 'You've done what?' he shouted, his voice harsh and sharp.

'I released Joseph Bunny last night,' repeated the sheriff, his words quiet and measured.

Carlson strode to the back of the office, past the deputies and down the corridor to the back room to where the small iron cage was neatly stacked with furniture.

'Son of a bitch,' came the shout from Carlson, as it echoed back up the narrow hallway. 'Son of a bitch.'

As Carlson turned to stride back, his foot hit a metal mop bucket, tipping it to clang and clatter across the floor, spilling dirty water on to his boot and trouser leg. 'Son of a bitch.'

When Carlson emerged back into the office his anger and fury was almost out of control. Will's hand instinctively went to the grip of his Colt.

'You released a murderer.' Carlson's words spat.

'Never proved,' responded the sheriff.

'Bunny killed one of my men and no one ever takes anything from me. Never. I'll get him, dead or alive, it makes no difference to me.'

'Maybe you will and maybe you won't. It's a big place down there, with a lot of places to hide.'

Carlson stepped in close, but Will didn't move an inch. 'You want to pray that I do find Bunny because if I don't I'm going to bring my men back to Eureka Falls and let them loose, in retribution for double-crossing Black Jack Carlson.'

Will dismissed the threat with a shake of his head. 'Best you be on your way, Mr Carlson, as there is nothing here in Eureka Falls for the likes of you and your men.'

Carlson turned and strode towards the door, his eyes dark with rage. Will glanced over at the mayor, who was visibly shaking, then slowly released his grip from the handle of his pistol.

20

A Matter of Conscience

Friday 7 June 1878 — Late Morning

The sheriff and his deputies stood on the landing outside their office and watched the eight riders leave. The sound of the hoofs upon the road made a low rumble as the dust kicked up to haze behind them.

'Riding hard,' observed Doogan.

'Stripped down too,' said Lonny. 'I guess they figure they will have Joseph by tonight or tomorrow.'

Will looked across at the horseless buckboard and the large coffin of Victor Kerry that now lay abandoned in the street.

'Doogan, will you go and get Cyril? He will need to take the body back.'

'I'll do that,' offered Lonny, his voice

almost a whisper.

'No, Lonny, I'd like you to go down to the stables and get my horse and saddle it up.'

'You going somewhere, Sheriff?'

Will looked back down the street, the riders now lost from sight. 'I'm going after Joseph to give him a hand.'

'But — ' Lonny seemed lost for words before he lifted his chin and drew in a breath. 'I'll go with you.'

'No, Lon, I need you to stay here and protect the town.' The sheriff looked over at his young deputy. 'You'll be the town's sheriff while I'm away. What I've got to do is a matter of conscience, my conscience, and no one else's.'

'How long?' asked Lonny. 'How long will you be away?'

'I'd say no more than a couple of days. That's all this will take, whichever way it works out.'

'Do you want me to saddle a second horse for you?'

'No, just fit the saddle-bags, all I

need is water and ammunition. And fit the rifle sleeve.'

Lonny turned to go.

'The one that fits the Sharps,' said Will.

Lonny jerked his head back to look at the sheriff. 'You taking the Sharps rifle?'

Will nodded. 'I want to leave here within the hour and I need to tell you a few things before I go, so if you could do it now, Lon?'

'Yes, of course. Right away.'

★　★　★

Within the hour Sheriff Will Price lifted himself into the saddle but as he rode out of town it was with a heavy feeling of unease. Part of it was the certainty of the danger he faced as he knew the odds were poor, very poor, but the uneasy feeling went beyond a fear for his safety. He knew the feeling of fear well — it had stayed with him during the war — but this time it was more than just apprehension. There was also an emptiness in his stomach as if he had lost something that he cherished. In less than a week his world had taken a tumble. From just Monday to Friday his life had passed from the quiet duties of a small-town sheriff to a head on collision between right and wrong. But what was right? And what was wrong? If that wasn't clear, he thought, then am I a fool?

Had Will fallen into Joseph Bunny's trap to take on Black Jack Carlson? Had he been foolish in not arresting Bunny for the murder of Victor Kerry, and for not transporting him back to Lake City himself — to hand him over to Wes Nettleton to deal with? Was that what he should have done? Handed the problem back? If he had, what would have happened? 'They would have hanged Joseph Bunny,' he said aloud, as he glanced to the left and right of the street to the familiar shop fronts of the town he called home.

Will flicked the reins and his horse broke into a trot as he pulled down on the brim of his hat. His left hand dropped down to touch the butt of the Sharps rifle, to check that it was secure. As he did, Mary Platt gave him a wave from the gate into the schoolyard, but he didn't see. Sheriff Will Price was looking ahead, lost in his thoughts and he didn't turn to look back.

21

A Shootout

Saturday 8 June 1878 — Morning

The Carlson gang was riding hard and leaving clear tracks as they headed south along the banks of the Las Animas towards the border. The sheriff followed behind at a trot and, as night fell, he dismounted and walked his horse to close the gap. This was his old army training kicking in and while these were lessons learnt some time ago the memories were still strong and clear. Walking also got the circulation back into his legs and eased the ache in his back after some six hours in the saddle. It also took the weight off his horse and kept her fresh, but most importantly it didn't let him ride into Carlson's overnight camp by mistake. So Will stepped out at a quick pace with the reins in his left hand as he checked his Colt with his right and listened for any telltale sign of eight armed men with killing on their minds.

Just before midnight he stopped and watered his horse from the river while refilling the two canteens he'd used that afternoon. He then walked some thirty yards directly into the brush to find a night camp on sandy ground near some Apache pines. He sat upon the horse blanket, his back against his saddle with his legs outstretched, and on his lap he placed his Army Colt with all chambers loaded and the hammer pulled back ready to fire.

By the time first light had broken the horizon he was up and walking again and, within the hour, he had found Carlson's overnight camp. They too had slept rough then departed at speed, leaving deep imprints in the sand where their horses had been raced in pursuit of Joseph Bunny. Will was now close behind as he mounted and dug his heels in to speed his bay south-west towards Bent Canyon.

Forty minutes later the ground on each side of the trail began to gently incline. Another thirty minutes on, the entrance to the canyon could be seen with its tall vertical sides. He stopped his mount and pushed forward in the saddle to listen, expecting to hear gunshots, but all was quiet. As he strained to listen he wondered if he had arrived too late. Had Carlson already caught up to Joseph Bunny and killed or captured him? Or had Joseph changed his plans and decided to make a run for the Territories? It would be a relief if he had, thought Will. Once Bunny and Carlson crossed the border it would no longer be his problem, or so he was telling himself when he heard the crack of the first rifle shot from deep within the ravine. It must have been Bunny commencing the engagement and Will wondered if Joseph had been able to reduce the odds by taking down one of Carlson's men with his opening shot.

Will pulled his horse to the right then whipped the reins with his wrist against her neck, letting out a, 'Ya, ya, ya,' to drive her up the embankment on to the rocky spur. She responded, thumping her hoofs into the ground to kick shale and stone high into the air behind her. Once on the ridge he turned her sharp to the left to follow a narrow animal track to the top of the western wall of the canyon. This was the most direct route as it skirted the scrubby uneven ground, but it was also dangerous to negotiate on horseback as the track was perilously close to the edge of the sheer drop to the bottom of the canyon.

As he rode on, gaining height, his horse wanted to veer away from the edge, but there was nowhere to go. They had to stay on the narrow path to get to the top. Will leant forward and put his head close to her neck and offered words of encouragement, while his heels kept digging hard into her flanks, willing and demanding her to respond.

When he got to the top and the grandeur of the long narrow canyon opened before him, he could hear the rifle shots clearly as they cracked through the dry air. He stopped, dismounted quickly and walked his horse some ten paces in behind two large rocks. The mare's eyes flashed and saliva hung from her mouth as Will settled her with hand pats as he released the belly band on the saddle. He then ducked under her neck and pulled the Sharps rifle from its sheath while telling her he'd be back.

The fire from Carlson's men now signalled that this was a shootout. He crouched and ran to the rim of the canyon to see a figure some 200 yards away on the opposite spur. Will dropped to fall on to his side then rolled into a lying position, close to the edge, the Sharps cradled in his right arm. He searched again for the figure he had seen, finally picking it out halfway up the ridge, crouching with a rifle in his left hand and a pistol in his right.

Will squinted into the bright light as he looked further up the ridge trying to find Bunny's position, which he guessed was probably just below the top of the spur, but Joseph seemed to be lying low. He eased forward and looked over the edge, down into the canyon, dislodging some small pebbles that cascaded into the void and down to the bottom some forty yards below. He scooped the edge back carefully with his left arm so that it wouldn't happen again. He then looked down to see where Carlson's horses had been corralled towards the entrance of the canyon for safety, behind an embankment against the far wall. One man, crouching near the horses, held a rifle. On the ground just behind him lay a body on its back with legs splayed at the end of two long marks where it had been dragged. It confirmed to Will that Joseph had indeed drawn first blood, so the odds were now six to one with one of Carlson's men dead and one left to mind the horses. Will drew in a breath and could feel his heart pounding as a voice inside said now is the time to reduce the odds further.

Will considered shooting the man with the horses as it would have been a relatively easy shot with a clear line to the target, but that man was not in the battle or causing any danger to Joseph, at least not at the moment. His first shot was important and had to have maximum impact both as a lethal shot and surprise, as his entry into the battle would effectively open a new front. His arrival however, would not only threaten his opponents, it would also put his own safety at risk. Those in his line of fire would quickly seek cover and find it difficult to engage Joseph, but they would also try to identify and engage him as a new target.

Another puff of smoke expelled from a small scrubby bush below and to his right on the far ridge. Will made a mental note of its position, then, a little further forward he sighted two men working together, moving up the ridge. He pushed the Sharps rifle forward and slid his body back a little so he could bring the optical sight to his eye. He sighted on one of the men then lifted the sight picture up the edge of the ridge along their line of advance. He was almost to the top when he saw Joseph fire from behind a small outcrop of rocks. Will now knew the position of the man he needed to protect.

He tracked the sight back slowly down the ridge and a new figure came into his view, moving slowly, rifle in hand and within twenty yards of Joseph and nearly level with his position. Will pulled the butt of the Sharps rifle from his shoulder and pushed his right hand deep into the side pocket of his jacket. In his fist he withdrew six .52 calibre rounds and let them drop to the ground next to the rifle. He thrust his hand back into his pocket and drew out another four rounds, which he laid next to the other six, lining them up neatly in a row. He picked up the first round, blew on it to remove any dirt and loaded it into the breech, pulling the hammer to the rear to cock the rifle ready to fire. He slid the butt back into his shoulder and placed his eye close to the end of the long brass optical sight that extended to the end of the barrel and began to search for his target. The man he'd seen advancing on Joseph couldn't be found through the sight's narrow field of view, so he lifted his head, glancing above the telescope, scanning his eyes across from Bunny's defensive position. He found his target, now fifteen yards from Joseph's position, bent forward in a crouch and moving with stealth.

Will pressed the sight back close to his eye, the figure was now fixed in a small circle and intersected by a thin black horizontal line. He bought the aiming point on to the forward edge of the moving target and lifted it to the area of the upper chest. The tip of the sheriff's finger slid over the trigger to the groove of the first joint as he drew in a breath. The target was now ten yards from Joseph. He breathed out a little, then stopped, holding his breath as he gently squeezed.

The rifle bucked as the large cartridge exploded with a thunderous echo and the heavy bullet fired from the muzzle on its flat trajectory across the canyon. Will kept his aim as he watched the projectile strike its target with a thump, collapsing the human figure instantly like a child's discarded rag-doll. The body rolled on to its back, head down but face up and began to slide down the steep slope through the undergrowth, twisting and curling as gravity pulled it towards the edge of the canyon, where, for just a second it seemed to hang before tipping over the edge and into the deep void. It fell, legs splayed and arms waving, almost as if floating, to finally hit the ground below with a sickening thud.

Will didn't dwell on the spectacle or

rejoice in his success. He had the second round in the breech, re-cocked and was now running the sight back down the ridge to the scrubby bush looking for his next target. But his entry into the battle had caused his foes to go to ground. So he aimed at the centre of the bush where he had previously seen rifle smoke and squeezed off his second shot. The Sharps rifle echoed its presence again into the canyon and Will quickly loaded the third round into the breech. He selected the same point of aim, took it to the right, one sight width to where the bush was thickest and fired again.

Almost instantly a man dashed from the bush like a startled rabbit, running crouched, before falling and tumbling down the ridge as he tried to get away. The fourth round chambered into the breech with a metallic ring as Will quickly reloaded and twisted his body to bring the sight on to the fast moving target. His quarry flashed in and out of view behind bushes and rocks before he caught sight and fired. The rifle kicked and the bullet struck a rock just inches above the target's head, splintering shards of shale into the air.

'Damn,' said Will out loud as he reloaded and glanced over the sight to find the target and refixed his aim. The running man now seemed to have lost his rifle, as both hands were waving in the air at shoulder height. Will tracked his target, keeping the sight picture moving at the same speed as the target that now appeared and disappeared through the brush. His victim was nearly halfway down the ridge when Will fired his fifth shot. The bullet struck the man down low, dropping him to his knees but it was not a mortal wound. He continued to scramble on all fours until he was out of sight behind a large rock.

The sixth shot he fired near the horses, into the open ground of the canyon floor to raise a spray of dirt and dust. This was a warning shot to the minder of the animals, who had already gone to ground and couldn't be seen, but Will wanted to ensure that he stayed behind cover and out of the battle.

The last three shots were fired back up the ridge, at likely hiding spots to the front of Joseph's position, to discourage any assassin who may have got close, but it failed to flush out any opponents. The tenth round went into the breech but it was not fired. It would be ready when needed, to engage a target of opportunity.

Will tucked the Sharps rifle into the cradle of his arm, pushed himself upright and stood back from the edge of the canyon, so that he could only be seen from Joseph's position, high on the opposite ridge. He held the rifle aloft so that it would identify him, not just as a friend but as Sheriff Will Price from Eureka Falls with his Sharps rifle. Will then turned and with short fast steps started to make his way back down the narrow track to the entrance of canyon.

Will was about halfway down the ridge when he heard horses riding out of the canyon at speed but he couldn't see them. They were tucked in close to the near wall. By the time he got to the bottom and was standing on the canyon floor, all there was to see was dust. But he took up a position in behind some jagged rocks and waited, just in the hope that a straggler would emerge and present a target. Now was the time for a little patience, he told himself.

22

Link Up

Saturday 8 June 1878 — Towards Noon

The sheriff of Eureka Falls remained in his hidden position at the entrance to Bent Canyon for just on an hour — waiting, listening, observing and ready to engage any target that came into view. But all remained quiet as he sat in silence and contemplated just how many of the Carlson gang had escaped from the ravine. He had no way of knowing who remained, either dead, wounded or lying in wait like him and also looking for a target.

He guessed that the man he had shot, the one that had tumbled into the canyon, would still be lying there in the dirt along with the other body he had seen near the horses, the one he presumed Joseph had shot during the opening engagement. The man he wounded could still be lying low and, depending on the severity of his wound, still dangerous. The final possibility was that one or two of Carlson's gang had remained in the canyon armed, lying low and ready to fight.

Each of these prospects gave rise to a dozen or more possibilities and all were dangerous, but this was no time to let the imagination run away. When that happened it could lead to a feeling of being overwhelmed and paralysis would follow. So Will dwelt on the passing of each minute, knowing that time diminished the odds of seeing the opportunity of a target. Now, he told himself, was the time to move and try to link up with Joseph but that required him to act with more than a little nerve — he would have to expose himself as he moved across the open canyon floor and up through the brush on the far ridge.

Will transferred the Sharps rifle to his left hand and drew his Colt from its holster. He then lifted himself up into the kneeling position and selected the point to where he would make his next move. He chose an oblong rock that would offer good cover once he got there. He sucked in three deep breaths then slowly counted down. 'Three, two, one, go.'

Will took off, crouching low, counting his steps as he ran. On the thirty-seventh step he was there, back down on to one knee with burning lungs from the short, sharp exertion. He held his position, sucking air into his heaving chest as he looked for the next bound, the next leg of his journey. On the count of three he was away again to his next selected position and this he repeated as he made his way up the far ridge, expecting at any moment to see a foe or hear the crack of a bullet — but the canyon remained quiet.

By the time Will neared the top of the ridge the muscles in his legs were aching and he could feel the sweat rolling down the centre of his back. He was unable to pinpoint the exact location of Joseph Bunny's position but guessed that he was about thirty yards away. As he edged forward he started to call out in a low voice, 'Joseph, it's Sheriff Will Price.' On the third call he got a response from a nest of rocks, a little higher up and to the right.

'Sheriff, up here.'

Will glanced up, still unable to see Joseph until he saw a waving hand just to the right of the rocks. He advanced quickly, calling as he went, 'Coming to you, Joseph.'

When he clambered in behind the rocks, out of breath and wet with sweat, he found Joseph sitting in a small clearing with two rifles and two pistols at his side, and a row of cardboard boxes to his front, each opened to expose the shiny rows of cartridges.

Joseph grinned. 'I would have come down and got you but this knee of mine is turning into a real nuisance.'

'Good view,' said Will, as he sucked in the air.

'Chose it myself. You can see right down to the mouth of the canyon.' Joseph looked across at Will as he lifted a canteen towards him. 'Water?'

Will nodded. 'Mine's over on the other ridge with my horse.'

'Is she drinking?'

Will drank deep from the canteen. 'Not unless she can unscrew the cap.'

'Then we need to water her soon.'

'She may have to wait a little longer until we see if any of Carlson's men are going to get in the way. Did you see how many men rode out?'

'I'm not sure, they were kicking up a lot of dust but I think it was five or six.'

'Five or six,' repeated Will. 'I've seen two dead and I wounded one, but I don't know how bad.'

'I think I killed one and I wounded another,' said Joseph.

'Well, I can confirm that you killed one, they dragged his body back down to where they corralled the horses. So if five or six rode out, then maybe there's just one wounded man out there lying low.'

'Or maybe none,' said Joseph.

Will rubbed his chin in thought. 'I'd expect them to counter attack before last light.'

'Expect so,' said Joseph. 'That would make sense. So why did they leave the canyon?'

Will shrugged. 'I don't know, but if they have a wounded man out there, they would want to come back for him.'

'Maybe,' said Joseph. 'That would be the honourable thing to do but — ' Joseph didn't finish; he just sat and looked out down the canyon.

Will broke the silence. 'But what?'

Joseph kept looking straight ahead. 'These aren't honourable men, even to their own kind.'

23

Secure

Saturday 8 June 1878 — Late After-noon

Will and Joseph sat in silence, perched high up on the ridge near the top to the canyon, looking and listening for any sign of Carlson's men. Not a word passed between them for well over an hour as the wind blew softly up from the valley floor to flick the small wild iris just to the front of their position. Each man sat, straight backed and alert, shifting his gaze over the terrain of scrubby brush to the left and right, then out to the middle ground and again to the left and right, then on to the entrance of the narrow valley in the far distance. This was the approach route over which an adversary would have to travel if they wanted to attack, and Will felt secure in their ability to defend this small position as Joseph had chosen well.

Every ten minutes or so Will raised the Sharps rifle to his shoulder to look through the optical scope and search for any sign of movement, especially along the edges of dead ground where a small force might be able to assemble with safety from view or fire. But all remained quiet except for the rustle of dried leaves as a small collared lizard scooted his way towards the two men to finally perch on Joseph's boot, one claw on the edge of the stitching where the sole had been repaired. It tilted its head as if to examine the strange sight and was surprised when a hand slowly reached down and rubbed the knee. The lizard spun on the boot, then looked back before it sprinted to the safety of the brush.

'Be dark in an hour,' said Joseph. 'If they want to use the light to take us out, then they better make their move soon.'

A hawk came in low over their position, its wings spread wide and motionless, except for the fine flared feathers at the tips, as it drifted slowly down the ridge searching for prey. Will watched the bird descend towards the entrance of the canyon to make a slow graceful turn and then land upon the top branch of a small dead spruce. Will kept his eye on the hawk for well over a minute before he spoke.

'They're not coming.'

'That's what I am starting to think,' said Joseph. 'But it makes no sense.'

Will lifted the rifle to his shoulder and looked down the telescopic sight at the bird. The hawk was now preening itself and in no hurry to move, folding its wings and seeming to settle and rest. 'That bird is telling us that there is no one close by.'

'So where have they gone?' asked Joseph.

Will rubbed his chin. 'Don't know.

There is only one route of advance on to this position and we have it covered, so if Carlson wants you, he must cross this ground to our front.' Will kept rubbing his chin. 'And he should have kept this position under surveillance in case you decided to withdraw.' He paused and tapped his chin. 'Unless . . . '

'Unless?' asked Joseph.

'Unless they have given up.'

'That doesn't make sense does it?'

'No, it doesn't make sense. Unless . . .' The word came out slowly and Joseph turned his head towards Will.

'Well, what?' asked Joseph.

'They want to draw us out.'

'What, to get us to follow them, so they can ambush us? It would have to be a good reason for us to do that. We are secure here.'

'Secure,' repeated Will, his finger pressed against his chin. 'He knows we are secure while we are in this canyon, that we can defend ourselves and that he is going to lose men trying to take us out. We've turned the odds against him and he doesn't want to fight on our terms. If it was you on your own, Joseph, he would have stayed and waited until you were fatigued then squeeze in on you from the left and right of this ridge, moving up in two groups, but he now knows you've got reinforcements and he might think it's more than just me. He might think I have at least one deputy with me and with those odds we could shoot down his men one by one.'

'So where has he gone?'

Will jerked his head. 'Jeezus. You fool, Will Price.'

The movement caught Joseph by surprise.

'What is it?'

'Eureka Falls.'

'Eureka Falls? You think they are heading back to Eureka Falls? What could they want there?'

'Me,' said Will. 'It's not just you they want now, it's also me. I need to get back to Eureka.'

'I'll go back with you,' said Joseph, as he shifted his weight on to his good knee and knelt up.

'You'd be better off taking your horses and running for the border, you'll be safe there.'

'I'm not chasing safe. I was never going to cross into the Territories; this canyon was as far as I intended to go; this was where I was going to confront Jack Carlson. But if he's run back to Eureka Falls, well then, I'll follow him because this has to be settled one way or the other.'

Will looked at Joseph, the lean farmer from a small valley north of the mountains, dressed in a frayed shirt and with a coating of yellow dust upon his unshaven face. But what he saw was a man of principle and courage who could put other men of a higher status to shame.

'I'll head down the ridge,' said Will. 'You keep an eye on me just in case there is someone out there. I'll signal if it is all clear then I'll go back up the far ridge and fetch my horse. Then you fetch yours. I'll see you down at the canyon entrance.'

Joseph nodded as he continued to search the ground to his front.

'Any trouble,' continued Will, 'and we meet back here and we'll stand together.'

The lines around Joseph's eyes showed a smile that he was trying to hide from his lips as he now knew this was no longer his fight alone.

24

Ambush

Saturday 8 June 1878 — Evening

Will knew it was dangerous to stay on the trail that led from Bent Canyon back to Eureka Fall, and to also stay on his mount as light fell, but he told himself that there was no choice. If he and Joseph were to dismount and walk their horses, or move cross-country in the dark, it may keep them from the danger of being ambushed but it would also slow them to a snail's pace. And, right now, Will knew that a hare's haste was required.

Joseph could see the urgency that was biting at Will, making his movements jerky, a little like that of a horse when it feels the halter for the first time. So he sat upright and ready for trouble with his rifle lying across his lap and held by his right hand.

A small brass buckle on a saddle-bag clicked to the rhythm of the ride, giving a gentle metallic ring above the muffled sound of the trotting hoofs upon the sandy track. Will twisted in the saddle to reached back towards his left side, to pull the strap tight and quieten its call. As his hand grasped at the fastener his shoulder dropped and his head tilted down, not by much, maybe just an inch or two, when the lightning crack of a rifle shot rang out through the dark and knocked the hat from his head.

Will instinctively ducked and rolled to the left, sliding, then falling from the saddle to land on the sandy ground, his upper right arm taking most of the impact before pitching on to his stomach. The second shot was high and came from the same direction, which was now behind him as he was facing back down the track. He spun around towards the line of fire and realized that his Colt was in his hand yet he had no recollection of drawing it from the holster. His finger slid across the smooth trigger and he was of a mind to fire into the dark, but there was no target so he held his shot while desperately searching for the location from which he and Joseph had been ambushed.

He could hear the horses off to the right cracking the dead wood of the brush underfoot as they stamped off the track but he couldn't see them. Then a low whistle came from that direction and Will knew immediately it was Joseph calling to his horses to stop and settle. The sound brought a volley of rifle fire, some four or five shots that cracked then thumped with loud thuds as the bullets struck the sand. Without thinking, Will took to his feet to use this diversion to his advantage and ran crouched for less than twenty steps across the pale surface of the track to a position behind a waist-high grey rock.

'Did you get him?' came the call from the dark about ten yards to Will's front.

'Don't know,' came the response. 'Pretty sure I got the first one. I saw him drop from his horse.'

'What about the second one?'

'Think so. I think I got him too.'

'Did you see anyone else?'

'No, just the two.'

'You better go see.'

'Maybe we should wait. Wait until first light.'

'No. We need to get the horses. We don't want them wandering off. I'll cover you from here.'

Will pressed himself to the rough stone surface not daring to move a muscle as his hand squeezed around the handle of his Colt. His mind raced as his eyes searched the dark desperately trying to identify the threat he and Joseph faced. It seemed to Will to be just two men, one giving orders and the other reluctant to obey.

Will waited, still searching for his opponents when he heard the sound of a boot scuffing against the rock just to his right, alerting him to the faint outline of a body sliding down over the sloping surface not more than a dozen paces away.

'I can't see anything yet,' came the call.

'When you do, you shoot,' called the other voice. 'You shoot and make sure they are dead, but don't go scaring the horses.'

'Well, how am I going to do that?' came the mocking response as the figure slid to the ground then let out a groan as his feet struck the ground.

Will could now see the silhouette of a man who limped as he stepped forward awkwardly and slowly into the dark. He was about to raise his revolver and aim, when without warning the figure was knocked to the ground with a thud, followed by the frantic sound of blows from hand and fist. It was Joseph who had jumped the man who had been sent to kill him.

'Harris, you all right? Harris?' came the call from up in the rocks.

But there was silence.

'Brooks, what's going on? Harris Brooks, talk to me.'

But the silence of the night had returned to the dark except for the distant chirp of cicadas from the underbrush. Will held his position and eased himself upright to see if he could locate where the voice had come from. When he was finally standing erect he thought he could just make out the dark shape of a head protruding above the rocks, but the longer he looked the less sure he became. Was it just another boulder, one of many and part of the rocky outcrop? He strained his eyes to see if he could pick up a clearer view, but was still not convinced, so he lifted his right foot on to the rough surface of the rock and eased his weight up, while keeping his eyes fixed on the dark shape.

It moved and Will froze, holding his breath, watching as the shape of the head bobbed up then down. He slowly lifted his Colt and extended his arm as he aimed at the dark form but before he could take aim, it disappeared. He edged further up the rock, now on his hands and knees, creeping forward up the steep surface, each movement deliberate and ready for his target to reappear before him.

When he was almost upon the point where he believed his prey now lay in wait, he stopped to listen. The stillness of the evening seemed to sit around his ears like a turned up woollen collar, pulled tight and muffling every sound. Will felt exposed, visible and vulnerable. He wondered if someone was behind him, lining him up in their sights, when just to his right only a yard or two away a figure stood up and called out in a low voice, 'Harris Brooks, where are you?'

A shot split the air like a whip crack and the bullet ricocheted off the surface of the rock with a high-pitched zing. The caller jumped back in fright, half turning to his side as if trying to get away, only to strike the edge of the rock

and fall towards Will who spontane-
ously lifted his left hand as if to help.
But when he felt the cloth of the jacket,
he grabbed a fistful and pulled with all
his might, dragging the man towards
him and off balance.

'Oh, shit,' came the call from the
stumbling figure as Will jerked with his
left hand and at the same time thrust
his Colt into the folds of the jacket, the
muzzle striking hard into the ribs.
'Omph,' came the call.

'Drop whatever you have in your
hands,' yelled Will. 'Drop it now, or I'll
shoot you dead here and now.'

The clatter of a rifle against the rocks
was heard above the heavy breathing of
the man as Will's face pressed close to
the back of his prisoner's head. 'Both
hands.'

'My other hand's free. My gun is in
its holster.'

'You leave it there if you want to live.
Now slowly lift both hands high to
where I can see them.'

The coat bunched up on the man's

back and touched the side of Will's face as his prisoner lifted his arms into the air.

'What's your name?'

'Bryant. Gavin Bryant.'

'Who's with you, Bryant?'

'Just Harris Brooks.'

'No one else?' Will's voice was strong and mixed with menace.

'No. Just the two of us but I don't know what's happened to him.'

Will went to speak when Joseph called from the dark, no more than a dozen paces away. 'I got him here.'

'You OK, Joseph?'

'I'm fine, Will.'

'And Brooks?'

'Out cold but with a gun against his neck.'

'We'll come down to you,' called Will. 'OK?'

'OK,' said Joseph as if responding to a daily work task.

Will twisted his grip on the back of the jacket and pushed at the same time to force Bryant to stand. The man let out a groan and seemed to buckle at the knees. 'Stand tall,' said Will.

'I'm wounded. Lost blood, been feeling light-headed.'

'Where are you shot?' The clipped words spat from Will's mouth without any sense of sympathy.

'Back of the leg, high up. Brooks is wounded too.'

'Where?'

'Low, on the foot.'

Will pushed at Bryant's back and he stumbled. 'Edge yourself up on the rock, then slide down to where Brooks is lying.'

With difficulty Bryant stood, breathing heavy and leaning on to his right side as he eased himself down over the rock.

'Coming to you, Joseph,' called Will. 'And I have my gun on him.'

'I can see,' called Joseph. 'If he tries anything I can shoot him from here. And this time I won't miss.'

Bryant groaned as he cautiously slid down the rock. 'I'm not going to do anything,' he called through laboured breaths.

Will pushed the back of Bryant's jacket, his body slipping down the last few feet to the sandy track to buckle and crumple to the ground. Will slid down to land with a thump at the feet of the lying figure. 'So where is Carlson?' he said, as he knelt down and pulled the handgun from Bryant's holster.

'He gone ahead.'

'Ahead where?'

'Eureka Falls.'

'How many with him?'

'Three.'

'Who?'

'Patterson boys, Bill and Sonny. And Dan Barrett.'

'The others?' said Joseph.

'Len Marlow and Tom Hart are dead. They're back in the canyon.'

'So you two were left behind to ambush us. Is that right?'

'That's right, but we had no choice.'

'What do you mean you had no

choice?' said Joseph.

'Black Jack put us here and took our horses. He said after we had killed whoever came out of the canyon, we could take their horses and follow him up.'

'He left two wounded men behind without their horses?' said Will. 'With no way of escape, except if you killed us and took ours?'

'That's right.'

'That's one way of giving a man an incentive to kill,' said Joseph. 'A wounded man out here without a horse could die.'

'Are all the others OK?' asked Will.

Bryant pushed himself up on to his knees and nodded. 'Is there just the two of you? We thought maybe more, at least another one,' said Bryant.

'Just the two of us,' said Joseph.

'I knew we shouldn't have gone after you,' said Bryant. 'What Moose did was wrong.'

'Amazing how a wound and capture leads a man to reflect on the error of his ways.' The sarcasm in Joseph's voice mocked at Bryant's confession. 'So what now, Will? Do we shoot them, or hang them? Shooting is a lot easier and I can do it from here without even having to stand up.'

Bryant let out a quiver, betraying his fear.

'No, we can't do that, Joseph, it would be against the law.'

Bryant moaned and sank further towards the ground with relief.

'But I feel duty bound to impound their guns for thirty days. After that, they can retrieve them from my office in Eureka Falls.'

Joseph rolled the unconscious Brooks on to his back and undid the buckle of his gunbelt, then stood. 'And?' he said.

'And we push on to Eureka Falls. On our own.'

'You can't leave us here,' cried Bryant. 'We've got no horses and we are close out of water. We are both wounded men. You leave us out here and we'll die.'

Will turned his head and spat. 'Then you better pray that your master, Black Jack Carlson, will come to your salvation because the good Lord won't.'

'Have some mercy, Sheriff,' called Bryant.

Will stood in silence.

'There's a limit to mercy,' said Joseph. 'I'd reached mine when I took off after Victor Kerry, Black Jack Carson and anyone who rode with him. Seems the sheriff has reached his too.'

'We'll die,' pleaded Bryant.

'Then,' said Joseph, 'that's the way it is meant to be.'

25

Vengeance

Sunday 9 June 1878 — Morning

They had been in the saddle all night, no longer fearful of ambush and able to make good time. The flat sandy trail by the river offered easy going for the horses as they trotted in the cool air to a constant swaying rhythm. Joseph insisted that they stop every two hours to check and water the horses, especially while they were close to the river. Will abided to this demand as it allowed him to dismount and walk in small circles, arching and rubbing his back to ease the dull pain low down and close to his left hip. His scramble over the rocks to get to Bryant had seemed to aggravate this nagging irritation and added to his discomfort.

It was only just before first light that Will felt the heavy hand of tiredness start to pull on his eyelids; before then, the ambush had stirred his blood to keep him wide alert and on edge. But with the rising sun came the soreness of the eyes that felt dry and gritty to the bright glare. To close them was an instant relief but also an invitation to sleep, if only for an instant, to then wake with a sharp jerk of the head and a feeling of guilty embarrassment that something as petty as drowsiness had won over self-discipline.

Joseph saw the smoke before Will, who seemed lost in his thoughts as they rode towards Eureka Falls in the morning light. It was just a grey smudge, sitting low on the horizon, a sign that the farmer knew and feared each summer season — fire. When he brought it to Will's attention, riding up close to him and calling his name twice, Will at first seemed a little confused.

'Smoke,' said Joseph.

Will glanced up.

'Over to the left of Spanish, sitting low across the ridge.'

Will shifted his gaze, turning his head slightly to search to the left of Spanish Peak, his eyes following the edge of the skyline. 'Smoke?' he repeated.

'Not a lot, so maybe it's under control.'

Will now sat erect in the saddle as he looked ahead, then murmured, 'Jeezus, that's Eureka Falls on the other side of the ridge behind Spanish.' He kicked and flicked his reins to bring his horse from the trot to a canter and lifted himself a little higher in the saddle. Joseph pulled his mount in close to Will's side.

'How far, Will?'

'Fifteen miles, maybe a little more.' Will didn't shift his focus from the horizon as he spoke.

Joseph went to speak again but held his tongue. He was going to say that it was probably just a burn off, someone clearing a block of land and getting rid of the unwanted brush, but he knew such a tale would be a lie. Only a big fire could put enough smoke into the air to climb out of the valley and over the ridge, and it could only come from one place. He patted the neck of his mount then glanced over his right shoulder to his second horse as it followed on a short lead. They had both been watered in the last hour so he felt comfortable with the demands that would now be made upon them, because from here there would be no stopping, not until they reached Eureka Falls.

* * *

The acrid smell of the smoke filled their nostrils as soon as they topped the ridge. It hung in the air to then penetrate into the mouth and leave a sour taste on the back of the tongue. The trail turned from the high ground to pass through the fir trees and then twist down into the valley, giving teasing glimpses where Eureka Falls lay below. But it took another twenty minutes before they made it to the grass clearing that looked directly over the small town.

Will stood in the saddle as they emerged into the open, the sunlight filtered through the haze that hung above them. As they rode forward to the edge of the ridge Eureka Falls came into view and they stopped. Before them lay the remnants of clutter and confusion. From this point they could look down the length of the main street shrouded in a smoky mist from the ruins of burnt-out buildings. The street was strewn with items of furniture, some stacked in piles but most scattered indiscriminately, with chairs lying on their sides, along with tables, wardrobes, filing cabinets, benches, barrels and the other trappings of commerce and domestic life.

Joseph switched his gaze to Will who seemed to be in a state of shock, his mouth open and his chin quivering as he took in the scene of devastation.

Joseph wanted to say something, anything, a word of comfort, but none came to mind so he sat back in the saddle and patted the neck of his horse, waiting for Will to lead off and into Eureka Falls.

* * *

Joseph followed behind Will as he rode at walking pace into the main street. He watched as the sheriff surveyed the ruins, turning his head to the left and right as his horse weaved between the clutter that covered what was the wide central street of the town. Some buildings had been razed to no more than a bed of dark ash, while some had been saved but with telltale black stains above the windows that told of the destruction inside. And yet miraculously some had survived except for blistered paint upon their outside walls where they now stood next to a vacant block where a building had once stood. But this random survival came with no rhyme or reason. The church at the top of the street had survived but the schoolhouse had not, leaving just its white surrounding fence untouched. Wilks Undertakers was completely gone. On the road to its front where the large building had once stood, was a stack of empty polished coffins that had been saved but without their lids. The haberdashery was also gone, to be now marked by a lone dressed store dummy in a blue silk dress that had once stood in the front window. The raised hem of the dress had been hitched up from the dirt to expose the central wooden stand with its three carved legs. The general store had survived but the telegraph office next to it was gone, as was the barbershop where a small box of scissors and combs lay in the street to mark where it once stood. But it was the sight of a metal cage standing amongst the ashes that fixed Will's gaze. He seemed to let out a quivering sound through trembling lips as he rubbed his hand across his chin. He was looking at where the office of the sheriff of Eureka Falls had once stood. It was completely gone, leaving just bare black ground and the skeleton of the cell that had once housed Joseph Bunny.

'Sheriff,' came a voice off to Will's left. It was Doogan, his face marked with black streaks, his shirt torn at the shoulder and the tin star on his chest hanging askew. 'We lost Lonny. He went back into the office to save the weapons but he didn't come out.'

Will jerked his head towards Doogan but as he went to speak, he choked.

The silence hung in the air before Joseph intervened and spoke. 'Where is he? Where is Lonny now?'

'With the others behind the church. Doc Larson has set up a makeshift mortuary, but I wouldn't go there, it looks bad, real bad. Especially Lonny,' he said before finally adding, 'I took him up there myself.'

Will pulled his horse around to face back up the street towards Joseph, who watched as the sheriff's face pulled tight, his lips clenched white and his eyes squeezed shut. When they finally opened they were glassy red.

'I gotta go see Lonny,' he said.

Joseph looked across at Doogan and nodded his head to signal that he would go with Will, who had started to walk his horse back through the jumble of saved items that littered the street.

★ ★ ★

A large green canvas sheet had been spread upon the ground behind the small white church, giving the impression of a large picnic blanket. Close to the back wall of the church was a row of white-shrouded figures, nine of them, all in a neat line. Doctor Mervan Larson stood in the centre of the makeshift area, apron on with his sleeves rolled up and talking to Cyril Wilks.

Will slid off his horse and walked towards the two men with faltering steps. Joseph followed and as they

182

passed a small group of townsfolk, who stood and stared, Joseph could sense their anger. When Cyril looked up and saw them both, his eyes narrowed and he turned and walked away while Mervan twisted on the spot to face Will, then slowly extended his hand but it was a muted greeting. 'Sheriff,' was all he said.

Will took off his hat before he shook the doctor's hand. 'How many?' he asked.

'Eight here and four still missing, two are children.'

Will cast his eyes towards the line of shrouded bodies. 'I count nine?'

'One is Victor Kerry. His body was with Cyril when his premises were razed, so I had the remains recovered and brought here.'

Will nodded slowly. 'When did the fire start?'

'After midnight when most were in their beds. Seems the fire was started in four different locations at once and most of those who died were overcome by smoke while they were asleep. Fortunately, that would have made it a merciful death.' He then added, 'Of sorts.'

Will dropped his head as he put his hand to his face, pressing a thumb and finger to the bridge of his nose. 'Lonny.' He drew in a breath. 'Deputy Sheriff Logan Pitkin. Is he here?'

'Yes, Will. Doogan and Cyril brought him to me just now. It was Lonny who alerted the town of the fire by shooting his pistol into the air. If he hadn't it could have been worse. Much worse. He started to pull the weapons out of the magazine but the smoke got to him too. It's smoke that's the real killer, never the flames.'

'Can I see him?'

'You don't want to do that, Will. Best to remember him as he was.'

Will lifted his head and shook it gently. 'No. I need to see him. I owe him that.'

'He's at the end, the one with the number nine at his feet. He's been burnt. Real bad.'

But the words were falling on deaf ears as Will began to walk in stumbling steps towards the covered bodies. Joseph followed some five or six paces behind, then stopped as Will knelt next to the white sheet that hung as if there was a frame suspended over the body to hold the fabric aloft. Will slowly bent down and lifted the cloth up then pulled it back to reveal the gruesome sight. Two blackened outstretched arms without hands pointed skywards from the charred body, which lay on its back. The features of the burnt mass were indistinguishable except for the white of bared teeth, now fully exposed in a hideous grin. On the chest was a yellowed, twisted tin star. Will seemed to buckle forward to pitch on to both knees, his head hanging low as he began to sob in uncontrollable spasms that shook his whole body. Those around stood perfectly still in silence and watched the desolate and pitiful sight, including Joseph who was the first to turn away.

It was then that Joseph made the decision to leave Eureka Falls immediately. He knew he could do nothing to help other than to leave. His presence would be a reminder of how all this had come to pass. It was he, Joseph Bunny, who had bought the body of Victor Kerry to their town just one week ago. What they didn't know was the shame and guilt he now felt, as it had been his plan to lure Carlson to follow, in the naïve hope that the town would rise as one and help him avenge his sister-in-law's death.

He could now see that it was an ill-considered plan based on nothing more than hope. It was also an irresponsible act of negligence that had produced devastating consequences on people he'd never met. In just seven days the simple and honest lives of this small settlement had been turned to despair.

Joseph tried, briefly, to tell himself that it was Black Jack Carlson, not he, who had committed the crimes here. But he knew better as the self-reproach returned, bringing with it self-doubt that smothered and extinguished the fire of vengeance and righteousness, and along with it the desire, the strength and the confidence to pursue Carlson. He knew he had lost and his will to fight had gone, at least for now.

★   ★   ★

When he went to bid farewell to Will, he wanted it to be a quick goodbye. He found the sheriff in the stables, over at the end stall where the sunlight shone through the gaps in the wall, picking up the dust and smoke in thin blue shafts that seemed to encircle the man and his horse. Joseph thought that Will was dressing down his mount until he realized that he was pulling down on the buckles and straps.

'You coming with me, Joseph?' Will's voice was strong and he didn't turn as he spoke, taking Joseph by surprise.

'You going after Carlson?'

'All four of them and in no particular order; they are all guilty and I will administer justice to each and every one of them.' The words came out with weight, as the belly strap was tightened to the click of the buckle.

'I've done enough damage,' said Joseph.

'You and me both but what's done is done. Now we have to clean it up.'

'I was a fool, Will, and this is all my doing, not yours, best I leave things be. I need to attend the farms, maybe after that . . . ' Joseph paused. 'Maybe after that . . . ' He paused again. 'I'm spent. I want to go home.'

'Home?' said Will. 'Then it seems that I have to do this on my own.'

Joseph hung his head. 'What do you plan to do?'

'Follow them to Lake City and if the sheriff there won't help, I'll shoot them down myself, even if I have to do it in the main street and hang for it after.'

'I'll ride with you, at least to my

farm. Maybe you'd like to rest over-night there, then we can decide.'

'No time for that, Joseph.' Will kept his back turned. 'They are already eight to ten hours ahead. For Carlson this was vengeance against me. But now it is my turn. And I want retribution.'

'I'll ride with you anyway.'

'Suit yourself.' The words showed no sign of emotion. 'But I'm about to leave now and I'm not waiting for any man.'

26

Decision

Sunday 9 June 1878 — Mid Afternoon

When Joseph left Eureka Falls, Will had already departed. The delay had come from necessity when changing the load from Heather's horse on to his own and saddling her horse as his mount. In his final inspection he noticed Heather's horse, Calico, lifting her rear foot slightly to the point of the hoof before placing it back down. Joseph ran his hand down the length of the leg, pressing gently to see if it caused any discomfort. It was fine, the trouble was the shoe itself had fractured and been lost on one side, leaving her unbalanced. He cursed himself for not making such a fundamental check and quickly examined each hoof of the two horses. All the other shoes were in various states of wear and OK, but OK was not good enough for Joseph, especially if a hard ride was called for over tough terrain, so he set to work with speed and skill to reshoe the two horses.

The luxury of hot shoeing was not available as the blacksmith's forge at the livery stables was deserted, as was the small office, except for a young boy who had been sent to mind the store for his uncle. So Joseph sifted through the trays of spare shoes, selecting what he needed and with a mouthful of nails silently and skilfully set to work. The boy stood and watched, receiving an unspoken lesson in the art of cold shoeing.

When he had finished, Joseph placed the tools back on to the bench, took the unused nails and placed them back into the metal tray and paid the young boy five dollars. It was more than was required for a service he had administered himself but without the facility of the stable he would have risked an injury to his horses and that, Joseph knew, must be avoided at all costs.

When he rode out of town he did so without looking back and it made him feel uneasy. He half expected someone to shout out abuse or even ride after him, to bring on a confrontation, but nothing happened, so he rode the horses to a gallop as he pursued Will towards Lake City.

But the demons had not been left behind in Eureka Falls. Lonny's face was now inside Joseph's head and the young deputy sheriff, with the sense of duty and a love for his town, was calling for answers and Joseph had none.

The main trail to Lake City followed the valley and Will's tracks were clear upon the ground. He was riding at a canter and would be making good time, too good for Joseph to make up the lost hour, so he took a lesser trail that made towards the high ground and the pass, in an attempt to meet Will as he came out of the valley. It was a chance that he had to take, albeit a slim one, but he had to at least make the effort to ride with Sheriff Will Price.

Towards last light as he emerged back on to the main trail, he quickly dismounted to search for recent sign. In the near dark it was difficult to tell and the ground was hard, giving little indication, when his horse turned her head back down the track and let out a snort. Joseph looked up and saw the shape of a man, dismounted and walking his horse. It was Will.

As he approached, Joseph lifted his hand in greeting but not a word passed between the two men as Will continued to walk on in silence, so Joseph fell into step behind him and followed into the fading light and up the steep trail to the top of the pass.

It was close to midnight before Joseph finally laid a hand on the sheriff's shoulder and felt him jump slightly with surprise.

'We need to rest, Will.'

'That can wait.' The reply was stern.

'It need not be long, but you need to rest up a little. We still have a full day's ride ahead and in the light we will make good time. You'll catch up with Carlson, of that there is no doubt but it may not be tomorrow or the day after but you will catch him.'

'That I will,' said the sheriff, but when he spoke he did not make eye contact with Joseph.

'So, rest. You need to be alert for when that happens.'

Will let out a grunt that seemed to acknowledge Joseph's plea.

* * *

On rocky ground amongst the fir trees on a small bed of brown needles the two men sat around a small fire. Neither felt hungry but Joseph cut some thin strips of salted beef and handed it to Will along with a tin cup of black coffee. The aroma was strong but not just from crushed coffee beans. Joseph saw Will sniff at the brew, his eyes squinting slightly.

'It's rum. I carry a small bottle to keep out the cold in winter. I was introduced to it by an Englishman who had lived in South America. Me, I'm not a drinking man and can take or leave alcohol but it has its purpose and this is one of them.'

Will sipped from the cup then tilted his head in agreement.

'What Carlson did to Eureka Falls was all Carlson's doing, not yours.'

Will said nothing at first, while keeping the cup close to his face. 'You believe that?'

'I have to,' said Joseph.

Will's face showed no response.

'Had I done nothing, had *you* done nothing, Black Jack Carlson would still have eventually made it to Eureka Falls.'

'You want to tell the people of Eureka Falls that?' asked Will.

'Not now, they're hurting too bad to listen but it's the truth.' Joseph sipped from his cup and felt the warmth of the rum burn inside his chest. 'Eureka Falls may have been saved for a time but eventually Carlson or someone like him, would have ridden in to take the spoils of a thousand men's hard work. That's how people like Black Jack work. They have no conscience, no principles, they see themselves as above the law and believe that all men can be bought, and bought cheaply.'

'Well maybe it's now time to put a stop to that.'

'That's what I was trying to do,' said Joseph. 'But the stunt I pulled was madness. I know that now and I have learnt my lesson. So you be careful, Will. You shoot Carlson down, or any of his men without reason, and you leave yourself open. You need the law on your side. Carlson will deny that he torched Eureka and will pay lawyers to prove it.'

Will finished the coffee from his cup. 'I'll be leaving when I wake, which I expect to be around four. What you do is up to you. It's your decision.'

'Yes,' said Joseph as he finished the last of his brew, 'it is.'

27

The Parting

Monday 10 June 1878 — Morning

Weariness had overcome Will and it was Joseph who woke first, just as the sky started to streak grey with the first light of a new day. He called to Will but he didn't respond. 'Time to be on our way,' he said and shook the shoulder of the crumpled figure.

Will jolted with a start. 'What was that?'

'It's coming up to light, time to go.'

'What time is it?'

Joseph unbuttoned the top pocket of his jacket and took out a battered pocket watch. 'Says a quarter before five but I expect it is after five. This timepiece gets slow.'

'You need to get it fixed then,' said

Will as he shook his head then lifted himself up on to one knee.

'No need, I hardly use it.'

'Why do you carry it then?' Will was looking down at the ground, still groggy from heavy sleep.

'Luck. It's been lucky for me. Carried it right through the war.'

Will looked up as he squeezed a thumb and forefinger to the bridge of his nose. 'You don't look like a man who believes in luck.'

'Oh, I believe in luck all right. Saw too many men survive by chance and there was no reason to it, they were just lucky.'

'But all luck runs out eventually,' said Will as he stood slowly.

'Yeah,' said Joseph. 'I guess it does.'

*   *   *

They rode most of that morning in silence with Will leading, bent forward in the saddle, displaying his sense of urgency. Joseph followed behind, close, his second horse with the supplies on a short lead. The trail travelled through the Wet Mountain Pass and along the far ridges, cutting through large stands of Douglas fir that ran dark green down into the valley on either side. The trail was well worn and suitable for a light wagon, provided there were no mishaps, as the edge fell away in a steep drop that could pull a team of horses and their driver non-stop to the bottom.

A late-morning meal was a brief affair and taken at Joseph's insistence so that the horses could be watered from a small cascading stream that fell from a sheer rock face to pool next to the trail. Joseph handed a slice of salt beef to Will, who nodded his appreciation before he walked up the trail, kicking his left leg out to ease the pain in his back. As Joseph checked the horses he noticed that Will's mount should have also been re-shod before the journey and went to say something but decided against it as

Will seemed preoccupied with his thoughts.

By mid-afternoon they were close to the turnoff that lead down the Arapahoe Valley to where Joseph's farm lay.

'I'll be turning off soon, Will. I need to attend to the farms. If you come with me we can rest up then leave for Lake City together. It will only put you a day or two behind.'

Will seemed to grunt his disagreement to the proposition.

'Your horse needs shoeing.'

'It can wait until I get to Lake.'

'I'll stand with you, Will, but I must see to the animals first.' The words were said, but not with enthusiasm or conviction. In fact, as the words came out, Joseph had to suppress an uneasy feeling inside.

Will didn't respond so they rode on for the next half-hour in silence.

When they came to the junction in the dip of the ridge, Joseph drew his horse up close. 'I'll be leaving you, Will.

I will follow in a day or two.' Then added, 'If you want.'

'No need,' said Will. 'I'll look after this myself.'

Joseph glanced around, not wanting to make eye contact in case his sense of relief was visible. 'When you do, do it by the law, Will.'

Will glared at Joseph. 'You telling me to do it by the law?'

Joseph caught his gaze. 'Yes, I am. You are the law. What I did was personal for what was done to family, to our Heather.'

'And I don't have that right? Even after what Carlson did to Eureka Falls?'

Joseph wanted to say no but he buttoned his lip as he felt like a two-faced preacher, the sort who had driven him away from religion.

'Let's just call it reckoning then,' said Will.

'I just don't want to see you hang for the murder of Carlson. If that happens, then he wins. Don't you see that?'

Will's face showed no emotion as Joseph extended his hand in farewell, but Will didn't take it, turning his horse to the flick of the reins to trot away up the trail towards Lake City.

28

I Didn't Squeal

Monday 10 June 1878 — Afternoon

Will rode away from Joseph as the pain in his back stabbed low on the left hip with each step of his horse. He was nearly thirty yards away before he pulled back on the reins and stopped, dropping his head to look down at his hands gripping the leather straps. 'Jeezus,' he said, then turned to look back down the track to where he had left Joseph, but all he saw was a glimpse of the horses as they turned off the ridge and down the trail. He lifted his hand to wave farewell, but Joseph was gone, leaving just dust amongst the trees. Will shook his head. 'You fool, Will Price,' he said out loud and thought of his grandfather. He flicked the reins and his horse started to walk, he flicked them again and she broke into a trot as he pressed his hand to his hip. The sheriff didn't look back but his thoughts of being a fool stayed with him along the slow rising trail to Lake City.

It was another two hours before he made it to the high ground that looked down into the long low valley that led to Lake City. To the right was the junction where the trail made its way east and down on to the plains and to Cheyenne Wells. Will dismounted and arched his back before he checked the harness and tightened the belly strap up a notch. As he pulled himself back into the saddle, he looked back over his shoulder and down the ridge over the way he had come, glancing to the left and into the valley where Joseph's property lay. All he could see was the dip in the trees in the far distance that marked its location, as the afternoon light turned the green foliage to a blue that seemed almost like a mist. He turned away and started to walk his horse then stopped again before turning in the saddle to take another look. The scene stretched back to the pass above Eureka Falls on the horizon and he glanced back toward Joseph's valley — something didn't seem right. He turned his horse to face back down the trail and walked her some forty paces to get a better view, then stood up in the saddle. He squinted into the low ground, searching the blue hue before it struck him what he was looking at. 'Smoke,' he said out loud and his horse snorted. 'Smoke in Joseph's valley.' He dug his heels in and his mount responded to his command and began to trot back down the trail, back the way they had come.

* * *

Will made good time coming back down off the ridge, but by the time he got to the turnoff to Joseph's farm it was almost dark. As he made his way down into the valley he started to pick up the smell of smoke and could see the embers of a near burnt-out fire some distance away. When he came into a clearing, Will thought that maybe he was in a holding paddock, some distance from the homestead, but ahead was a fence and gate that marked the entrance to the farm. From here he could see the outline of a barn, so he dismounted and began to walk his horse forward to the smell of resin from burnt pine.

Against the corner of the barn Will tied off his horse near a low wooden water trough, then slowly walked down past the closed doors. At the opposite corner of the barn he could see the outline of the farmhouse between two large trees, but there was no sign of life, not even the dim glow of an oil lamp from inside. So he stood, taking in the scene and wondering where Joseph might be, as the smell of the smoke continued to hang in the cool still air.

Will started to walk towards the

farmhouse when he thought he heard a sound, no more that a low murmur off to his right. He stopped and stood still, straining to hear but there was only silence, so he started to walk again, slowly. He was almost to the house when he heard it again, and this time he pulled his Colt from its holster and turned in the direction from where the sound had come.

As he walked across the open ground towards a large oak his foot struck something soft. He squatted down to see, feeling with his left hand, his Colt tucked close in to his right side. It was a dead chicken, its neck broken and twisted. Will slowly eased himself up and pulled the hammer of his pistol back till it clicked into place. As he did the sound came again from under the tree, an incoherent murmuring. Will edged forward and was almost to the base of the tree when he saw the dark outline of a figure half standing, seemingly propped-up against the trunk.

'Who's there?' he called.

He heard a low cough; one made with difficulty.

'Who is it?' he called again.

The response was muffled.

'Say again,' said Will a little louder, and this time he heard the answer.

'Joseph,' came the laboured reply.

'Joseph, it's Will.'

The word Will was repeated back but it was faint and mumbled.

Will stepped forward under the low branches, his foot striking another dead chicken, then another, before he was at the slumped figure. He leant forward as his left hand felt towards the object before him, his eyes searching in the dark.

'Jeezus. Jeezus, Joseph, what have they done to you?'

The figure of Joseph, half standing, half squatting was tied to the trunk of the tree, the rope bound around his chest and under his arms, to leave him hanging with his head slumped forward and turned to one side.

'Breath,' came the low voice. 'Can't get my breath.'

Will pulled at the rope around Joseph's chest that tied him to the tree; it was looped three or four times and as tight as a steel band around a barrel. He holstered his Colt and ran his hands along the length of the rope and felt where the knots were tied. His fingers worked frantically to pull them apart and he cursed as they defied his pinching and pulling until finally, an end came free. As the knots released, Joseph's weight pulled down on the loose rope and he slumped to the ground, drawing in short shallow breaths.

Will scurried back around the large trunk to Joseph. 'Carlson?' he said.

Joseph nodded. 'Burnt out Heather's property, killed most of the stock and were about to burn down mine when I came across them.' The words were laboured and Will had to lean in close to hear. 'I got one of them by surprise but I took a shot to the ankle and couldn't walk. The Patterson brothers jumped me from behind and Carlson had me tied to this tree.' Joseph licked his lips. 'Will, you got any water? I'm as thirsty as hell.'

'Sure, Joseph.' He turned to fetch the water. 'Carlson? Where's Carlson now?'

'Gone,' said Joseph as he coughed. 'But not to Lake City though, I heard them say Cheyenne.'

Will rushed back to his horse and pulled one of the canteens from the saddle and shook it, it was half full. When he placed it to Joseph's lips he drank with hunger but difficulty, spilling most of the water.

Will slid his arm around Joseph's waist ready to lift him. 'Got to get you inside so I can look at that wound, see if we can save your foot.' He tugged trying to lift the crumpled figure, but Joseph made no effort to stand. 'You got to help me here, Joseph,' said Will.

Joseph lifted a hand and placed it on Will's shoulder, but it was not to help him to his feet. The fingers just gave a gentle squeeze.

'They cut me, Will. They cut me real bad.'

'Cut you?' repeated Will. 'How?'

'Just like I did to Victor Kerry, but — '

Will put his hand down on Joseph's leg, the trousers were loose and wet with blood. He pulled his hand back as if he had touched a hot branding iron.

'But,' said Joseph, 'I didn't squeal. Victor Kerry squealed, but I didn't and it just seemed to make Carlson more angry than he already was.'

'Got to get you inside,' said Will.

Joseph's fingers squeezed again. 'No need, Will.'

Will placed his hand on Joseph's shoulder, his fingers squeezing a reply.

'Will.' The voice was now not much more than a whisper, low and soft but jagged with pain.

Will leant in, turning his head so that his ear was close to Joseph's lips.

'Will, I want you to take the

Schofield, the one I took from Victor Kerry. I didn't get to use it and it looks like a fine pistol.'

'I have a good pistol Joseph,' said Will. 'I have my Colt.'

'I know you do, but I want you to use this one. I want you to use this one when you kill Jack Carlson. When I took it from Kerry that's what I planned to do with it, but I never got the chance. It's my unfinished business but now it's yours.' Joseph drew in a breath with difficulty, 'It's yours to finish.'

Will nodded his head and patted the shoulder of the mortally wounded and mutilated man.

'Promise me that, Will. Promise me you will finish it, not just for what's been done, but for what Carlson can still do.' The words were said with urgency.

Will nodded again but Joseph seemed unconvinced.

'Promise me, Will. Promise me on your life.'

'You have that promise, Joseph, that I will bring Carlson and those who have served him to account for what they have done. I give you my word on that.'

Joseph's grip on Will's shoulder loosened then fell away as the air expelled from his lips, warm against Will's ear.

Will turned his head to look at the pale features of the man he had known for just one week, his unseeing blue eyes staring at him in the dim light. 'I promise,' he said and the words took him by surprise, as if they had been spoken by someone else.

★   ★   ★

Will took two oil lamps from the farmhouse and lit them to provide light as he wrapped the body in a blanket. But as he did, he averted his gaze from the large bloodstain that covered Joseph's trousers down to the knees. He removed Joseph's boots and took a clean white pillowcase from the bed in the small farmhouse and pulled it over Joseph's head in an effort to provide dignity to his fallen comrade.

He buried the body in a small depression at the back of the white-washed barn, where the earth was soft. He then placed two small timber planks flat on top of the mound to signify a cross and to mark where the body had been buried. Joseph's boots he placed together, neatly, at the foot of the grave. When he stood, it was well after midnight and he felt obliged to say something, a prayer maybe, but Will was not a religious man. That had left him years ago with the unanswered call to why his wife and child had been snatched from life, so he just repeated the words, 'I promise.'

He then took Joseph's personal possessions: a locket, his leather money purse, and the old battered pocket watch and placed them on the bed in the farmhouse. The Schofield he took as directed, wrapping it in a small blue cotton cloth that he found near a porcelain wash basin. As he made to leave the small home and go back to the barn, Will stopped briefly and held the oil lamp high to view a photograph on the mantel near the door. It was of a young Joseph in uniform, next to a slightly younger man also in uniform, which must have been his brother Linton. Will had a similar photograph of himself, taken just after he had signed up. Both men looked keen but a little grim. Maybe, thought Will, the stories from those who had survived the early battles had been whispered into the ears of these two young men. Stories where honour and courage were obscured by the fear and savagery of death and suffering. But whatever horrors lay before these two young farmers who had been called to arms to protect the Union, they had survived. It was what had followed after the war that was now to be questioned. Was this a nation where good would triumph over evil? Or do the efforts of all good men turn to dust?

29

The Chase

Tuesday 11 June 1878 — Morning

Will slept the few hours that were left of the night in Joseph's barn, propped against a large post with his Army Colt close by his side. But it was a fitful sleep laced with anger and guilt that woke to every creak of timber or snort from his horse. Before first light he made ready to leave and, as he pushed the large barn door closed, he glanced across to the tree where Joseph had been tied, mutilated and left to die. A chill ran down his back.

In the early overcast twilight of dawn he walked his horse to the gate that marked the entrance to the property, and in the half-light found the body of

Dan Barrett lying close to fence. The face was bloodied where Joseph's bullet had entered the right eye to cause instant death. Barrett had most likely been on guard at the gate when Joseph had arrived. After that, the telltale scuffmarks and blood-soaked earth close by showed where Joseph had been wounded and overwhelmed. Drag marks led directly across the yard to the tree.

Will looped a rope around Barrett's feet then mounted and secured the running end to the saddle and began to pull the body along the ground. He rode up the track at a walking pace from the farm and on to the ridge, to where it met the trail to Lake City. There he dismounted and untied the body that was now battered and dusty, with the shirt and jacket bunched-up high under the arms to expose white flesh. He left it lying, face up on the track with the arms extended above the head, and in the shirt pocket he placed a note:

This is the body of Dan Barrett. Please advise the sheriff of Lake City of its whereabouts and of his demise. He was killed by Joseph Bunny in an act of self-defence, before he too died at the hands of Jack Carlson and the Patterson brothers.

He signed the note, *WP, Sheriff Eureka Falls* and dated it, *11 June.*

As Will stepped over the body of Barrett, coiling the rope in neat loops, he was aware of his sense of detachment. The air was still and cool but he felt no cold. He had not eaten, other that a little salted meat the day before but he felt no hunger. He was committed to chasing three men with the intent of killing them but he felt no anger or fear. He had dragged the body of a dead man along the ground like the carcass of a discarded animal but felt no guilt or remorse. It was as if his emotions had been numbed like the fingers of a hand thrust into an icy stream. His feelings had frozen, removing him from what he could still see, hear and touch. It was as if he were alien to his surroundings, his own consciousness, to life itself.

This was not an unpleasant feeling and it caused him no apprehension or concern. He had been in this state before, during the war, after his first battle when he and his fellow survivors had been detailed to bury the dead. At that time the reality of death had cut each young soldier like a sharp blade but one that drew blood before it drew pain. He knew this feeling would eventually pass but at the moment it would also serve him well. He knew it was easier to kill when disconnected from the emotions of worry, remorse and fury, as it made killing a mechanical act. There would be no mercy, no leniency, no compassion for Black Jack Carlson and the Patterson brothers. He would avenge with efficiency and ease for what had been done to Eureka Falls and to Joseph, and he would do it as soon as the opportunity arose. It was the promise he had made not just to Joseph but also to himself.

As Will rode back up the trail to the turnoff to Cheyenne Wells he looked for sign on the ground, to show where Carlson might have passed but could find none. He wondered how he had not come across the three men the previous evening after they had left Joseph's farm, but that small mystery resolved itself not long after he passed the junction that marked the trail east to Cheyenne. A narrow track, just wide enough for a horse, joined from the right and clearly showed fresh sign of where three riders had entered the main trail. This minor track must have led back into the valley and to Joseph's farm and been familiar to Carlson. Maybe it was the very trail that Victor Kerry had taken to the farm when he went to collect the rent money from Heather Bunny and to ravage her.

Will had no way of knowing how far ahead Carlson and the Patterson brothers were at that time. He expected that they had rested up overnight, so estimated that the gap between them and himself was some four to six hours at the most. As he rode at the trot he considered the possibilities that were now before him, the possibilities that would arise when he finally came face to face with the three. The first was a confrontation on the trail before he got to Cheyenne but he felt that was unlikely, as it would be difficult to close the gap no matter how hard or long he rode. The second possibility, and the most likely, was a confrontation soon after arriving in Cheyenne. With luck he might be able to surprise them but that chance was also slim, as sooner or later Carlson would expect to be challenged and therefore remain alert. The third possibility was to seek assistance from the sheriff of Cheyenne Wells. This was what he should do, he knew that, but could he trust anyone in Cheyenne? It was the town from where Carlson had started, before he set his sights on Lake

City and beyond. Did the leaders of Cheyenne Wells all owe Black Jack Carlson? If they did, then was it likely that they would protect him?

'Not Luther?' Will said aloud. 'Not Sheriff Luther Doherty?' But Will didn't know the answer to this last question, so he told himself that if necessary he had to be prepared to do this on his own and accept the consequences that followed. And if those consequences included arrest and imprisonment, after shooting Carlson and the Pattersons in cold blood, then so be it. 'And,' he added, 'I have no intention of hiding that fact, even to a Colorado court of law.'

★ ★ ★

By midday the trail was down in the low hills and heading due east on to the plains. The tracks of the three horses were still clear to see, as were their frequent stops that were marked by boot prints. Carlson seemed to be in no hurry and by mid afternoon Will thought that he could see a little dust in the distance but he didn't dwell on the possibility that he was within striking distance of his prey. Ahead lay the wide lower reaches of the Arapahoe River that snaked to the south out of the Arapahoe Valley. The foliage on the banks was lush and thick, criss-crossed with a thousand intertwining tracks, where cattle and wildlife moved to the water's edge.

Will was undecided if he should spend the night at the river before riding through to Cheyenne when he noticed that his horse was constantly lifting her right rear hoof when standing still. Inspection showed that she had thrown part of a shoe and spiked the sole near the heel from a twisted piece of metal. Will prised the obstruction free with his belt buckle and decided to lead her on foot directly across country to the banks of the river and water her.

He was less than half a mile from the river when the sound of a single rifle shot in the distance made him stop with a jolt. It had come from the trees that lined the river but over to his right, some distance away, maybe as much as a mile. Will stood still, looking, straining his eyes to catch any movement. Was it just a fellow traveller looking for a cottontail to roast over the fire for his evening meal? Or was it Carlson and the Patterson brothers?

Will started to walk at a sharp pace straight towards the undergrowth of the river to make cover so that he could not be seen. As he did, he kept his eyes on the location from where the sound of the shot had come, expecting to catch sight of movement, even a figure, but all remained as it was, devoid of human sign or activity. But someone was there, at least one person, maybe three? Maybe it was Carlson and the Patterson brothers. Maybe he had caught up to the three men he was now hunting, maybe he was in a position to confront them on the trail, while he still held the precious advantage of surprise and was away from the prying eyes of witnesses. His mind raced ahead, his hand touching his Colt, checking that it was in place and ready for use.

Once into the shade of the trees and brush, Will felt secure from being seen. As he made his way towards the river-bank in the dappled light from the shade of the undergrowth, he searched for any sign of life. The water's edge was flat and open, reflecting the glare of the low sun up on to the underside of low branches that protruded out over the edge of the river. Will let his horse drink as he looked down the river towards a small open area of bleached sand in the distance. A splash appeared in the water to its front. Maybe a fish, thought Will. Then another. Followed by a third. Will kept his eyes fixed on the spot as, there in the distance, appeared a figure, stepping to the water's edge, to be followed by a second man and finally a third, who was just a little taller. All three were now standing and looking across the wide expanse of the shallow river. Another splash appeared in front of them as one of the men threw rocks to skip upon the surface of the water. Will felt his heart beating faster as he slowly edged back out of view to the safety of the brush.

He quickly pulled the Sharps rifle from the saddle holster. Then, propping on one knee, he lifted the rifle to view the three figures through the optical sight. This would be a long shot and out to the limit of the rifle, just over a thousand yards. Should he take it?

Will guessed that the probability of hitting a man-sized target with a first shot was about fifty-fifty, as he would not have the luxury of an adjusting shot from which to correct. And once he had fired the other two would go to ground and immediately seek the cover of the brush. Surprise would have gone but did that matter if he had killed his target? Even if he only wounded his mark, it might still give him an advantage, as the other two would now be slowed by having to care and travel with a wounded man — provided they chose to help. But the biggest question that hung over Will was the identification of the three men. Was the taller figure that of Black Jack Carlson and were the other two the Patterson brothers, or three different, innocent men?

He pressed his eye to the sight, straining to get a clear view and identify the three figures. His heart said it must be them but his head said it wasn't sure, not a hundred per cent sure. He had to get closer but he didn't want to lose the opportunity that now presented itself.

30

The Opportunity

Tuesday 11 June 1878 — Mid-morning

Will returned to his horse, tethered her, then pulled a box of .52 cartridges from the brown saddle-bag and dropped them into his jacket pocket. As he ran through the brush towards his targets, dodging, weaving and ducking under low branches, he counted each step. At 400 paces he turned abruptly to the left and ran to the water's edge to try and resight his target. They were gone.

He sprinted another 100 paces, counting aloud under his panting breath then cut back to the edge of the river again. He stopped, searching and trying to pick up the exact point where he had last seen the three men. Then from out under the trees, some 600 yards away three horseman appeared in single file as they commenced to cross the river at a walking pace.

Will dropped to one knee, close to the water's edge and lifted the Sharps to his shoulder, pulling the hammer fully to the rear to cock the weapon as he sighted on the first of the three men. It was Carlson he could see, he was now sure, leading on a black horse, upright in the saddle and looking towards the far bank.

'Son of bitch,' said Will aloud. 'Son of a bitch.'

The target was moving from his right to his left as he adjusted his sight to the leading edge of Carlson's chest. He sucked in three deep breaths to slow his breathing then expelled the air before drawing in once more, long and deep before he let it out again. With his left elbow propped just forward of his left knee he steadied the rifle and fixed the sight so that it was moving just slightly ahead of the target and slid his finger on to the trigger. Just as he was pulling back with a steady force, his target pitched out of view as the rider kicked his horse into a gallop, instantly disappearing from the small aperture.

'No,' called Will as he lifted his head to regain a view of the riders. All three were now at a gallop, splashing water high into the air as they bunched and turned slightly to the right, riding away.

Will lowered his eye back to the opening of the optical sight, catching glimpses of the riders as they bounced in and out of view. 'Damn,' he called in frustration. Then, the last of the three riders slowed his horse to a walk as the other two raced ahead. Will quickly readjusted his position, allowing his right boot to now lie flat in the sand of the river-bank as he leant back to rest his weight on his foot and steady his position. He placed the thin black sight line on to the third rider, sucked in two breaths, breathed out, stopped, steadied and with a soft pull, squeezed the trigger.

The recoil of the rifle kicked back

into Will's shoulder as the sound from the muzzle rolled across the open expanse of the river like distant thunder. For just a second or two nothing seemed to happen, then as if by delay, the rider fell from his horse and into the shallow river to lie perfectly still.

Will dropped the butt from the shoulder and pulled the lever of the rifle down, ejecting the spent cartridge to splash into the water by his side. He pushed his hand into his coat pocket and pulled out the cardboard cartridge box and tried to open it with one hand. But his fingers could not make a purchase under the lid, so he cradled the rifle in his arms to free up his left hand so that it could hold the box while he pulled and ripped the cover free with his right.

The sunlight flashed on the brass cartridges as they spilt and jumped from the box to fall upon the sand. 'Damn,' he called as he scrambled to pick up the rounds and return them loose to his pocket. The one bullet he retained he now blew upon to remove any sand but could still see where wet grains were clinging to the case. 'Damn.' He wiped the round against his shirt then slid it into the breech and pulled the lever back up into position and drew the hammer fully to the rear ready to fire again.

The first two riders had continued on at full gallop and were almost to the far bank before they slowed to a stop, to pause and wait. One turned his horse to look back, then slowly at first, started to make his way back towards the fallen rider. The other rider followed but some distance back and in no haste.

Will watched, glancing up from the 'scope to then look back down the tube at the small crumpled shape lying in the shallow water, then back to the two riders as they returned from the far bank. They must have heard the shot, he told himself. But their actions indicated ignorance as they rode, tall in the saddle, back into the killing ground.

It was only when the lead rider was within fifty yards of his fallen comrade did he speed up to a gallop to then quickly stop and dismount in a spray of water.

Will sighted on the figure as it bent over the man he had shot from the saddle, and carefully adjusted his elbow on his knee to support the long heavy barrel of the rifle. Once again he commenced his routine of drawing in long measured breaths as he sighted and prepared to fire. Although this target was smaller and low to the ground he was now confident he could take him out as he was static and he had assessed the range accurately. Will breathed out slowly, stopped, steadied the thin vertical black line on the still dark shape and squeezed the trigger.

The rifle bucked and Will lifted his head as he pulled down on the lever to eject the empty cartridge, while keeping his eyes on the target. It didn't seem to move and he wondered if he had missed as he searched for any telltale splash of the large round hitting the water. He loaded the next cartridge, lifted the rifle to his shoulder and looked through the scope at the target. It remained still. Will pulled the large hammer fully to the rear and glanced up to catch sight of the third rider who had now turned and was riding away at full gallop while leaning low in the saddle.

Will sighted on to the diminishing target as it bounced in and out of sight. To drop this man from his horse would be at best a lucky shot. The only chance was to take out the horse and force the rider to run on foot but with each second this was becoming more difficult. Will looked down the sight as he watched the target then squeezed off the shot. But as soon as the rifle fired he knew he had missed and as he lifted his head he saw the splash as the round struck the water just to the rear left of the horse.

31

Yes, It Was Me

Tuesday 11 June 1878 — Midday

Will didn't know which two men he had shot. Their bodies now lay in the distance some 600 yards away, collapsed and still, slumped together and showing no sign of life. As he trudged towards them, his boots digging deep into the soft sand of the river-bank, he hoped that at least one was Black Jack Carlson. If it was, should he take the body into Cheyenne Wells or back to Lake City, he thought? Or should he push on and pursue the third man, the one who had got away? His thoughts raced ahead with each step as he considered what he should do. He had identified Carlson as one of the riders but after the three horsemen had started their race across the sandy shallows of the river, he had been unable to tell who was who. One of those lying ahead was certainly a Patterson but which one? Was it the younger brother Sonny or was it Bill, the one with the reputation for meanness and violence? If it was Sonny who had escaped, should he be content to hand the job of justice over to either the sheriff of Lake or Cheyenne? If it was one of the Patterson brothers, would the other now come gunning for him?

Will trudged on then stopped abruptly and dropped his gaze down towards his boots as he rubbed a finger across the cleft in his chin. He was still 300 yards from the bodies but he knew instinctively who he'd shot. It was the Patterson boys, Bill and Sonny. A brother would not run out on his sibling and especially a Patterson. The rider who had escaped must have been Carlson who had run away. Black Jack Carlson was a survivor. Will looked back down the river towards where his horse was tethered, some 700-800 yards away, then turned and began to trudge back, following his footprints that were now starting to fill with water.

★ ★ ★

He found his horse standing quietly where he had left her, her rear leg bent and the hoof tilted forward. He ran his hand down the length of the leg to confirm that her tenderness was isolated to the hoof, then patted her rump and slid the Sharps into the saddle holster.

He walked his horse back out of the river brush and into the sunlight to turn left to parallel the trail to Cheyenne Wells. Three quarters of a mile up he found the tracks of the three horsemen cutting back towards the river. He followed them and found the ground where they had briefly camped and watered their horses. Directly to the front, in the shallows of the river, just sixty yards away were the two bodies.

Will checked his Colt, mounted, then slowly rode out to inspect what he had done.

He was within fifteen paces when one of the bodies moved. It was the one lying on his back, his clothes dark from the water lapping around him. He was pinned by the body of a larger man with a hole in his back, who now lay slumped across his legs. It was the body of Bill, the older brother who had returned to help his younger brother Sonny.

Sonny looked up at Will, his face white and with fear in his eyes. He had been shot through the side but the bullet had first entered his arm near the elbow, smashing bone and twisting it so that it now stuck out at an odd angle, as if pointing to something of interest. Small flecks of white splinters could be seen jutting out from the moist red wound. Sonny's belt had been pulled from his trousers and was strapped to the upper arm to act as a tourniquet.

'You,' Sonny said, as he looked up at

Will. 'It was you.'

'Yes,' said Will. 'It was me.'

'You got Bill too.'

Will nodded.

'He came back.' As Sonny spoke, small bubbles of blood appeared at the corner of his mouth.

Will nodded again.

'Bill's dead and I'm going to die.'

Will lifted his head and looked across the river to the far bank before he turned to look back down on the young man. 'Yes,' he said. 'You are about to meet your brother in hell.'

32

Let the Law Proceed

Wednesday 12 June 1878 — Morning

Will's horse could do no more than walk, so he dismounted and trod beside her in the cool of the night towards Cheyenne Wells. He felt calm and his sense of detachment stayed with him as he quietly contemplated what he would do on arrival at Cheyenne. He felt confident that his quest to bring Black Jack Carlson to account was almost at an end.

He walked right through the night with no sense of tiredness and entered Cheyenne with the first light of dawn, a lone figure, gaunt, unshaven and covered in dust that made him look much older than his 37 years. In the past ten days he had lost close to a stone in body weight but it was not just his physical appearance that had changed. Deep inside, Sheriff Will Price now felt an emptiness, a loss, as if something very important and personal had been taken from him but what that was exactly, he couldn't say. Was it the life of Deputy Sheriff Lonny Pitkin, whom Will had recruited and nurtured to be his senior deputy? Or was it the farmer Joseph Bunny, whom he had chosen to protect, even though he had broken the law? Or was it the other lives lost at Eureka Falls, a town that now lay wounded and in ashes?

The young boy at the CW Livery Stables accepted Will's lame horse and directed him to the sheriff's office, which had moved since his last visit to the town the year before last. Sheriff Luther Doherty had yet to arrive, so Will told the young deputy that he would wait on the veranda, where he sat in silence with his Sharps rifle and saddle-bag at his feet, as he sipped from his canteen.

Those who passed all looked, some nodding and mumbling a morning greeting but Will didn't notice as he stared straight ahead, lost in his own thoughts.

When Luther appeared, he welcomed Will with a firm handshake and slow smile. 'I thought I'd get to see you, I just wasn't sure when,' he said. 'You want to come inside? I'll get the boys to put on some coffee.'

Will nodded in agreement as he lifted the rifle up from where he had placed it flat on the floorboards of the veranda.

Sheriff Doherty picked up Will's saddle-bag to assist. 'Wes Nettleton sent me a telegraph,' he said as they entered his office to the ring of small brass bell above the door. 'It was regarding Victor Kerry, advising me that he was heading my way.' Luther motioned for Will to take a seat. 'Then Wes followed it up with the news that Kerry had turned up dead in Eureka Falls and that Carlson was on his way there. When I saw Black Jack ride into town last night I had a feeling that something had happened. He had near killed his horse he was in such a hurry. Got here just before the bank closed and withdrew a large amount of cash. I asked him what was going on but he said it was none of my business.'

'Well it's about to be your business, Luther,' said Will.

'I guessed that. You want to explain, Will?'

Will was about to make the statement that he was there to kill Carlson but paused.

And as he did, Luther asked. 'Coffee? I always find it best to discuss business with a friend and colleague over coffee.'

This small recognition of their relationship, both social and professional, unexpectedly touched Will. Although he didn't know Luther well, he was a colleague, a fellow lawman and a man he knew he could depend on. 'Sure,' he said, 'I'd like that, Luther.'

As Will cupped his hands around the

tin cup and sipped the strong black brew, he felt himself relax for the first time in what seemed an eternity. He knew he should talk and explain, tell his story, his grandfather would expect him to. So, he sucked in a breath and began, telling of the arrival of Joseph Bunny in Eureka Falls with the body of Victor Kerry the Monday before last, around midday.

Luther pulled the spindle-backed chair away from the desk so he could sit. 'That would be the third,' he said. 'Ten days ago.'

'Yes,' said Will slowly, 'ten days ago.' He stopped to think. Just ten days ago, is that all it was, he asked himself? Just ten days ago?

'I take it Bunny killed Kerry over the death of his brother's wife, Heather?' asked Luther.

'Yes,' said Will as he began to tell of the events of the last ten days.

★ ★ ★

When he had finished, Luther let out a 'Phew'. Then leant back in his chair. 'You and Bunny have taken down Carlson's gang. That leaves him on his own. This really does change things. Without those men Carlson will be unable to collect the rents. It could be over for Carlson.'

'No,' said Will. 'It's not over, but it will be soon. I've come to kill Black Jack Carlson.'

Luther shifted uncomfortably in his chair. 'That would cause me a problem, Will. If you kill Carlson in cold blood, no matter what the reason, I have no choice but to charge you and take you into custody for trial. But . . .'

Will straightened his back and fixed his gaze on the Sheriff. 'But?'

'But Carlson isn't here.'

'What?' Will's eyes creased as he pushed forward in the chair. 'Where is he?'

'He left on the night train to Topeka. It pulled out two hours late, around midnight, but I was there with two of my deputies loading a silver shipment from the First National and I saw Carlson leave. I now realize why he looked like such a relieved man. And from what you've just told me, I doubt if he is coming back.'

Will fell back in his chair. 'Gone last night? The train to Topeka?'

'I'm afraid so. I had no reason to hold him. Had I known, well . . . '

Will looked around, agitated. Then he slapped his hand on the desk. 'We need to telegraph ahead, get him held.' Will's voice was urgent.

'I can do that, but he'd be out of Colorado by now and into Kansas and we have no jurisdiction once he crosses the line. You know that. I can still raise a warrant for his arrest and send out a detailed description but who do we send it to? I doubt if he is just going to stay in Topeka. That train connects to Jefferson then heads north to Springfield.'

'Where do you think he will go?' asked Will.

'I'm only guessing, but I'd expect north to Chicago or even further east.'

'Further east? Where?'

'He has business contacts in New York.'

'New York?' Will slumped in the chair.

'I can get a general bulletin out so that it goes in the *Gazette*, but I doubt if we are going to see Black Jack Carlson again in Colorado for a long time. And that in itself is something to rejoice about.'

Will was unmoved, deep in thought as the empty coffee cup lay in his lap.

'What do you want to do, Will?'

'When is the next train to Topeka?'

'Night after tomorrow. You planning on chasing him down?'

Will stood and as he did, the cup fell to clang on to the bare timber floor, but he paid no attention to it, standing, fixed like a statue, as if frozen on the spot.

'You planning on chasing Carlson down?' Sheriff Luther Doherty asked again.

Will turned his head slowly towards Luther, his pale blue-eyes cold and staring into the distance. Luther frowned a little as he looked intently at Will, while the two deputy sheriffs who had been standing by the front counter showed their embarrassment at the silence by shuffling their feet and looking down at the floor.

'Stop,' said Will, his voice sharp. 'Don't make a sound.'

Both deputies jerked their heads up in fright, eyes opening wide from the reprimand.

'Can you hear that?' said Will.

One of the deputies opened his mouth but he wasn't game to speak.

'Hear what, Will?' said Luther.

'A train.'

'Train? No freight due in today.'

Both deputies nodded in agreement with their sheriff just as a steam whistle blew three times to announce the arrival of a train into Cheyenne Wells.

'Well that's certainly unexpected,' said Luther as he slid his empty coffee cup on to the desk. 'And it sounds like it is coming from the Topeka side. Pity. If it was going the other way, Will, you could have followed after Black Jack Carlson.'

The bell above the door rang to interrupt Luther as a silhouette appeared against the morning light. It was a young man in a railway uniform. 'Sheriff, Mister O'Hern sent me to tell you that last night's train to Topeka has returned. It has a leaking boiler and he would like you to come down straight away and escort the silver consignment back to the First National vault, just to be safe.'

No one in the sheriff's office moved, their eyes now fixed on Will.

'Sheriff?' called the station clerk from the doorway.

'Yes, Tim,' said Luther slowly. 'Tell Stationmaster O'Hern that I am on my way.'

'I'm going with you,' said Will, his hand on the grip of his Army Colt, fingers splayed around the handle as if ready to lift it from the holster.

'Will.' Luther stood and stepped forward, the palm of his hand held upright. 'I'm going to have to ask you for your handgun and rifle.'

Will's head spun to the side to fix his gaze on Luther. 'My guns?'

'Yes. For your own good. I can't have you shooting Carlson down in public. Too many witnesses for a start. Let me arrest him and let the law proceed.'

'Let the law proceed? What right does Carlson have to the law?'

'The same as Joseph Bunny,' said Luther. 'I'll take your gun now, Will.'

Slowly, very slowly, Will relinquished his grip on the Army Colt, his fingers still splayed as Luther leaned forward and slid the handgun gently from its holster.

'I will have to impound your rifle as well.'

Will nodded slowly. 'But I want to come with you.'

'Of course, you can be there when I arrest Carlson and escort him back to our lock-up.'

Will dropped his head then glanced across at his saddle-bag. 'My canteens and valise, can I leave them here, safe?' asked Will.

'Sure. Just put them on the other side of my desk. They will be out of the way there.'

One of the chastened deputies reached down to pick up the brown leather bag but Will quickly pulled the saddle-bag away. 'I'll take it.'

The deputy looked surprised and a little confused.

'If you could take my canteens, then that would be appreciated, but there is something in here that I need,' said Will as he gripped the valise.

33

The Promise

Wednesday 12 June 1878 — Mid Morning

Will kept his left hand in the pocket of his jacket as he walked alongside Luther and his two deputies towards the Cheyenne Wells railway station at the bottom of Seymour Street. The train could now be heard clearly, hissing steam and jarring metal against metal, as the rolling stock shunted into the siding.

When the four lawman passed through the covered alcove and on to the platform, the large black locomotive filled their view, appearing through a cloud of white steam that flooded over the timber boardwalk, obscuring the passenger cars, freight wagons and the red guard's van at the rear.

'A sorry sight.' The stationmaster, in his dark coat and pillbox cap, was examining his pocket watch.

'Problem?' asked Luther.

'Problem,' repeated the stationmaster. 'I just hope we can fix it; our workshop is not equipped for boiler repairs. The crew did well to get her back here, and they' — he nodded towards the passenger cars — 'are better off in Cheyenne Wells than sitting out on the prairie.'

'For most but not all,' said Luther, as he looked down the platform, his hands on his hips. 'I know of one who'll be none too happy about being back in Cheyenne, as I'm about to arrest him.'

The stationmaster's eyebrows rose above the small round rims of his brass glasses. 'So who would that be?'

'Black Jack Carlson,' said Sheriff Luther Doherty.

'Good God! Are you are going to arrest Carlson? On what charges?'

'Property damage' — the sheriff

paused still looking around — 'and murder.'

The stationmaster's walrus moustache pulled up at the corners of his mouth. 'Son of a gun — ' But his words were cut short as the train came to halt and vented a searing spray of steam from its side.

As the final wisps of white mist curled up to disappear in the station roof, the noise of opening carriage doors could be heard and the passengers began to alight.

Will stared hard at the passengers, the weight of his body now on the balls of his feet, in anticipation, should he need to pounce.

'Cheyenne Wells,' came the baritone call from Stationmaster O'Hern. 'All alight. All alight. Take your luggage, this train terminates here for repairs. This is the final stop, Cheyenne Wells.' The stationmaster turned to Luther. 'We need to attend to the bullion shipment and get it back under lock and key.'

'My deputies will go with you, Tom. I

have other business to attend to first.' The sheriff's head was held high as he glanced over the crowd. 'And it looks like I'll have to go and find Mr Black Jack Carlson.'

'Well, if you go on board, hang on,' said the stationmaster, 'as my boys will start unhooking and shunting the rolling stock before the engine is out of steam.' He then gave a wave of his arm to signal to the two deputies to follow, but they looked to Luther first for his nod of approval before they began to follow behind the large man.

'You wait here, Will,' said Luther, without taking his eyes off the tired and dishevelled crowd that now milled around the platform gathering up their luggage.

'I can't see Carlson,' said Will.

'He's here somewhere,' said Luther, 'but I doubt if he'll be in any hurry to step back on to this platform. Seems I'll have to go and get him.'

As Luther stepped off towards the first carriage, Will instinctively stepped with him, but Luther stopped and turned side-on in Will's path. 'No, Will, best you leave this to me. This is my business now.'

Will went to protest but before he could speak Luther was walking swiftly away from him, so he stood, his hand thrust deep into his jacket pocket clenching the smooth steel frame of the .45 Smith & Wesson Schofield revolver, while his heart raced in his chest. Then, with slow steps he began to walk forward against the flow of passengers who now shuffled towards him with their luggage, their shoulders bumping against his, knocking him slightly off balance while he looked up into the first passenger car where the sheriff was checking each empty seat.

To keep up with Luther, Will had to step out, only to be buffeted by more passengers as the sheriff's figure advanced across the open metal bridge from the first to the second passenger carriage. As the crowd continued to push past, Will felt a sense of panic as he could see that he was being left behind, so he thrust his right hand forward to help separate the bodies advancing towards him and clear a path, while his left hand continued to grip the Schofield. And all the time, his eyes remained fixed on Luther as the profile of the sheriff flashed and waved through the glass of the carriage windows.

As the last of the doors slammed shut, Will emerged from the crowd, now halfway along the third and final passenger car, just as Luther started to step down the small metal ladder and back on to the platform.

'Where is he?' yelled Will.

'He's not on board,' called Luther.

Will spun on the spot to look back down the station platform, his face grim and confused as he searched for Carlson, but there was no sign. He turned back to Luther. 'Are you sure?'

'You can see for yourself.'

Will pushed past Luther and pulled himself up the three narrow metal rungs and on to the open bridge of the third passenger car, his left hand still in his pocket. As he entered the dark carriage he had to pause, unable to see, so he clenched his eyes closed for three or four seconds then opened them as his heart thumped in his chest. Where? he said to himself. Where the hell are you, Carlson? But the carriage was completely empty as he looked down the long vacant aisle of the three connected carriages.

Will dropped his head and slowly turned to go, just as his eyes caught the flash of a long, dark, jagged shadow through the window to his left. It was moving to the rear of the train on the side of the carriage away from the station. Will leaped towards the window, one foot on the seat as he grabbed at the frame with his right hand to lower it open, but it wouldn't move. He rattled the window frame with frustration then pulled his left hand from his jacket pocket, still holding the Schofield. He tried again to lower the window but it wouldn't open, so in desperation he twisted his left hand and thumped the butt of the pistol against the glass, smashing it.

The sound of the breaking glass seemed to immediately hush the crowded station, as the window came free and dropped down with a slap, spilling the last of the broken glass from the frame. Will pushed his head and shoulders through the opening to catch sight of Carlson running with difficulty over the broken ground alongside the rail tracks, a large carpetbag in his left hand.

'Carlson! Stop!' yelled Will as he fumbled to transfer the Schofield from his left to right hand, nearly dropping it. 'Stop!' he yelled again, the handgun now held steady, his thumb pulling back on the hammer. 'Stop, or I'll shoot.'

Carlson stopped, looked back at Will, his face filled with fear. Then he threw the bag under the train to follow on all fours, scrambling out of sight.

Will instinctively fired at the disappearing target before he could aim, the shot splitting the air and echoing off the iron roof of the station. The bullet struck the stony edge of the sleepers just near Carlson's right boot to spray dust and gravel into the air. 'Damn,' said Will, as he went to fire a quick second shot but just as he did, the train jumped to jar him against the window frame. When he looked back out the window, Carlson was gone.

'Will,' came the call from the platform. It was Luther. 'Will, what's going on?'

'It's Carlson,' called back Will. 'He's gone under the train.'

'Will?' came the call again from Luther.

'Damn,' said Will as he stepped from the seat and on to the windowsill to look down at the uneven ground below him. 'Damn you, Carlson,' he repeated and jumped.

His left foot struck the edge of a railway sleeper, twisting and throwing him off balance, to pitch and fall on to his right side, hard against the steel rail of the parallel track. The pain in his ankle was like a lightning bolt, while the thump to his ribs was like that of a prize-fighter's fist, which expelled the air from his lungs in a whoosh.

Will wanted to curse but he couldn't speak. He couldn't even catch his breath as he lay on his side, stunned. Got to get up, he said to himself, but then a second voice followed, the familiar voice of his grandfather. 'Be careful, Will.'

Desperately he tried to suck air into his lungs, his mouth opening and closing, frantically gasping like a fish that had just been hauled to the bank. But the air wouldn't enter his lungs and he felt his vision narrow with the dark edges of unconsciousness. Help me, came the cry from the voice in his head. Help me, just this one time. And, as his vision went black, he saw his grandfather as clear as a picture, his face close, leaning in, almost touching him as if he were to be kissed. He relaxed.

The swimming, swirling black of this dream was a relief from the pain, so he relaxed to the sensation that felt like falling into a deep dark hole. But just when he thought he might hit the bottom, his grandfather's voice called out sharp and loud 'Will', and the air rushed into his lungs like a spray of steam. The dark edges of his vision disappeared and the sunlight flashed into his eyes, to reveal a large solid steel wheel as it jolted with a screech and the noise of unclamping hooks and falling chain.

Will rolled on to all fours and pushed himself upright, only to buckle as he placed his weight on to his left foot. The stab of pain was so excruciating that it made his jaw tremble but he forced himself to stand, desperately trying to take all of his weight on to his right leg. But when he stepped forward with the left foot he pitched and fell, jarring the fingers of his right hand that held the pistol on the jagged stones by the railway tracks. Do it Will, said the voice inside. You promised Joseph, and you can do this.

The train jolted again to the sound of screeching metal as Will, now on all fours, followed Carlson under the carriage and into that dark confined space below the train. In pain and cloistered fear, where the wheels rocked back and forth to the jolt of uncoupling wagons, he searched for Black Jack Carlson.

When he lifted his head to look forward, it struck the steel frame of the carriage, restricting his view; and when his left hand slipped on the oily surface of a metal pit cover, he fell flat upon his stomach, the left side of his face striking hard against the rough surface of a sleeper.

He lay there defeated and exhausted, sucking in shallow breaths and coughing from the dust and smell of rancid grease. Carlson had gone and he could only hope that Luther had seen where.

Will reached out slowly to the left and clasped the smooth steel rail with his free hand, close to the edge of a large silver-rimmed wheel and drew himself up, to get out from under the train. Now on all fours, he pulled his hand back, just in the instant that the carriage above his head jumped, as if hit by a violent blow that turned the wheels a full circle to the rear with a jarring crash, shunting the wagon back down the station.

Will froze, his eyes wide with fright as he realized how close he had come to having his hand severed by that rim of hardened steel. The force of the jolt continued to ricochet into the next carriage, then the next, cascading down through the rolling stock towards the rear van.

Then it happened.

An agonizing scream pierced Will's ears. It was a cry of tortured distress, a wail from a wounded animal but Will knew who it was. It was Carlson.

With clenched teeth he kicked and

pulled himself forward, crawling, twisting, squirming, dragging his body with all the strength and urgency he could muster. And in that dark dangerous space Will Price came upon Black Jack Carlson, his body wedged between the tracks, his head lying flat near the large carpetbag and the steel wheel straddling his groin.

Will pulled himself up into the narrow gap of the railway line next to Carlson, his body pressing close as he leant in near to Black Jack's face. Carlson's eyes were open wide and his lips trembling as Will placed his right hand on Carlson's chest, still clenching the Schofield, then moved it down towards his waist. The cloth of his trousers was sodden with blood and he pulled his hand back as he heard a muffled murmur.

Will strained to hear but the voice was no more than a whisper, laboured between short, shallow breaths, so he had to lean in so close that his ear was almost touching Carlson's lips. As he tried to listen, Will slowly slid the barrel of the Schofield up under Carlson's chin.

'You got me, Price,' came the muffled words, each separated by a small gasp. 'But it was only by luck.'

Will pressed the Schofield against Black Jack's jaw, his fist tight around the grip as his finger squeezed slowly on the trigger.

Carlson licked his lips and Will noticed the blue tinge against the pasty white of his face. 'Had this train not returned to Cheyenne Wells' — he licked his lips again and grimaced in pain — 'you would never have found me.'

'Luck?' whispered Will, as a small bead of sweat glistened and slowly ran down the groove of his chin. 'Luck had nothing to do with it. I would have found you, Carlson, somehow, some-where, someday.' The shiny drop fell from his chin and on to Carlson's cheek. 'Even if I had to go raking hell.'

'So,' said Carlson, his dry tongue

flicking the top of his trembling lip, 'it is almost over.'

'Yes,' said Will, as his finger continued to slowly squeeze the smooth black trigger of the Schofield revolver. 'It is almost over. I promise.'

THE END

Other titles in the
Linford Western Library:

HOMBRE'S VENGEANCE

Toots J. Johnson

After witnessing his father's murder at the hands of cattle baron Dale Bryant, fifteen-year-old Zachariah Smith grows up fast. Struggling alone to survive fully occupies his mind — until he meets two of Bryant's other victims. He realises that he must join the fight for justice and avenge his father's death, knowing that lead will fly and he will probably die trying to stop Bryant. But now Zac is a man, and it is time for the hombre's vengeance!

IRON EYES IS DEAD

Rory Black

Desert Springs was an oasis that drew the dregs of Texas down into its profitable boundaries. Among the many ruthless characters, there was none so fearsome as the infamous bounty hunter, Iron Eyes. He had trailed a dangerous outlaw right into the remote settlement. But Iron Eyes was wounded: shot up with arrow and bullet after battling with a band of Apaches. As the doctor fought to save him, was the call true that Iron Eyes was dead?

TAKE THE OREGON TRAIL

Eugene Clifton

Thousands of men had taken the trail to the west looking for a new beginning — many didn't make it. Adam Trant had also set out on the Oregon Trail — but he was looking for an old enemy. The hunt took him to a savage wilderness and matched him against deadly marauders. Adam was ready to die, as long as he succeeded in his quest. However, he wasn't ready for the unpredictable force of the love of a woman.

FOOL'S PLAY

Carl Williams

Royce rides into Jawbone looking for a doctor, but finds trouble. Living by the gun can he expect anything else? He signs on with land baron Yale Jamerson, hoping for a job that will leave his conscience clear. However, when Jamerson plans to dam the river and charge road tolls, the towns-people revolt. Forced to choose between his livelihood and his conscience, Royce must decide which path to take. Will it lead to a showdown with his closest friend?